# *New Cases of Sherlock Holmes*

***by***

**Janet Shaw**

First edition published in 2022


All characters appearing in this work are fictitious. Any resemblance to real persons, living or dead, is purely coincidental. The opinions expressed herein are those of the author and not of Orange Pip Books.

Hardback ISBN 978-1-80424-286-5
ePub ISBN 978-1-78705-959-7
PDF ISBN 978-1-78705-960-3

Published by Orange Pip Books
335 Princess Park Manor, Royal Drive,
London, N11 3GX
www.orangepipbooks.com

# CONTENTS

# The Case of the Mysterious Teeth

## The Case of the Mysterious Teeth

I struggled against the tide of pedestrians, all the while striving to keep the tall helmet in sight as the constable strode ahead of us, but I was losing the battle: buffeted and elbowed and quietly cursed, I was barely making headway.

"Watson! Make haste!" It was Holmes, his unusual height making him clearly visible above the strangers' heads, turning briefly to me as he marched forward, apparently unhindered by the crowd and certainly gaining ground.

"Holmes!" I called out. "Holmes, a moment!" In desperation I shouldered a looming navvy with some vigour and ducked forward, weaving my way closer to Holmes. When I reached his side, my tie was awry, I had lost a coat button and I felt myself lucky to still possess my hat.

"And here is our constable," I said to Holmes in some relief. "I thought I had lost him."

"I find that if I keep close behind him, I get on very well," said Holmes as we walked. "He creates an eddy much as a rock in the middle of a stream. It seems that our fellow foot travellers prefer not to bump a member of the constabulary."

We put our heads down and continued on our way, glancing up at the constable every so often to make certain of our way. I still clutched the note he had brought Holmes not ten minutes since. "Something in your line," it read. "Come at once. Morgue. Lestrade." I had barely had time to throw on my hat and coat as I bustled to keep up with Holmes.

We reached the broad, imposing steps of Scotland Yard, and I paused for breath before mounting them two at a time, still trailing Holmes and the constable. Once inside and shouldering through the busy vestibule past citizens of all walks and in all humours, we were led down a deep flight of stairs to the gloomy cellars that housed the morgue.

Lestrade greeted us. "You got my message all right, then?" He nodded to the constable. "Very good, Johns. Off you go." He turned to us with animation as the young policeman took the stairs. "I thought to myself you would very much like to see this one, Mr Holmes. I think you will agree that it is quite in your line. In here."

We followed him through a pair of heavy doors into a large, low-ceilinged room lit by at least a dozen new electric lights. Their illumination was so intense I was momentarily blinded but by the time I had followed Lestrade and Holmes to the far corner of the room I could see that we were approaching a table upon which a sheet had been laid. I could see that under the sheet lay a body.

Lestrade stepped to the head of the table and drew back the sheet theatrically. Revealed lay a young woman, pale in death, her eyes closed and her cheeks alabaster, altogether giving one the impression of a marble goddess, an impression only heightened by her bare shoulders, the delicate underclothes she was wearing and the luxuriant hair that tumbled over her shoulders. She was possessed of almost regal beauty.

"What dreadful misfortunate has overtaken this poor young lady?" I asked, moved by her untimely death.

"I rather fancy that the answer to your question is the reason we have been summoned," said Holmes, looking to Lestrade. "Well, my friend? What are we to observe? You rather have the advantage of us."

"And not the first time, I suppose," said Lestrade, but Holmes bore his needling impassively. "Well now, look here." Lestrade gently drew down the front of the woman's camisole to reveal two red spots just above the top of her corset. They were each the size of a pea and were circled in an angry red.

"Good heavens!" I exclaimed. "What dreadful thing has happened here? What has caused these marks?"

"Ah," said Lestrade, pointing his finger into the air with an expression of quiet triumph. "I am before you on this, Dr. Watson, Mr. Holmes. Clearly this is the bite of some deadly animal. Thus, I took the liberty of calling the head keeper from the London Zoo to help us identify the beast responsible. From thence we will be able to ascertain how it came about that she was bitten. I expect the keeper imminently."

Holmes leaned closer to the dead woman, his keen eye following the line of her camisole, observing her throat and arms, then gently touching her closed fingers. "Gripping," he said. "Possibly startled. No ring: apparently unmarried." He leaned in over her face and head for a moment, a slightly quizzical expression on his face. "No rigour as yet. A very recent death."

"That is certainly so," said Lestrade with a touch of professional pride in his voice. She was found at the service entrance of St Bart's Hospital not an hour since and brought here immediately." He looked down at the lovely face with an air that suggested the proprietorial. "Almost warm, this one, though bless me we don't know who she is."

Holmes continued his examination. "No violence to be seen here. Does your pathologist believe there was an outrage?"

Lestrade was astonished. "But this death was not by human hand, Mr. Holmes. You can yourself see the bite. This was not murder, so no, there was no outrage perpetrated upon this woman. As it happens, our doctor has not yet attended, but he will confirm what I say, I am in no doubt."

Holmes cast me an inscrutable glance. "As you say," he said quietly. "My mistake."

At that moment the young constable came through the doors followed by a tall and vigorous man dressed in indeterminate garb, neither that of a gentleman nor of a labourer. I took him at once for the zookeeper.

"I came immediately, sir," he said, glancing from Holmes to Lestrade. "I am Robert Morton, from the London Zoo."

Introductions were made and Morton was brought forward to examine the bite on the woman's breast.

"Well," said Lestrade. "What say you: viper? Wild cat?"

Morton had given an initial start on observing the dead woman. I felt some pity for him: familiar as he must be with death in nature, I hazarded that he was not so accustomed to viewing the corpse of a young woman. Even I still found that death had a way of seeming always at odds with the living, always ill placed. Morton gathered himself, and leaning in to examine the bite, was clearly perplexed. "I would say neither, but I am not sure I can say what creature was responsible for this cruel bite. Unless…" he stood upright. "I shouldn't like to suggest this, sir, if I could just see another solution, but I believe the only creature that could make a bite this big without savaging the skin is a vampire bat."

His words struck a chill through me, and I read alarm in Lestrade's face. He mouthed the word "vampire" apprehensively, for in recent months the London police had borne the heavy brunt of the near hysteria that had followed the publication of a lurid new tale of horror concerning just such a beast, but with human form and supernatural powers.

Holmes, however, retained his suave calm. “You think so?” he asked Morton mildly. “Your professional judgment is that this young woman was killed by a bat?”

“Well, I, that is, the bite …”

“Oh strike me,” said Lestrade suddenly. “Here I am forgetting the best part. Now, vampire bat or no vampire bat, what do you think of this?”

With a flourish he stepped towards the woman and reaching for her fist, prised open her still soft fingers to reveal in her palm a single arch of vulcanite and porcelain false teeth. “There!”

Holmes pounced upon the teeth and held them up to his eye. “Now we begin to see,” he said to himself, as he rotated the dentures for closer scrutiny.

“Well at least we know it has no bearing on the case at any rate,” said Lestrade. He moved to the woman’s face and gently opened her lips, revealing her teeth. “Not hers, you see. It was just a novelty I thought would amuse you, Mr Holmes.” He turned to the still flustered Morton. “I thank you sir, for clearing up this little mystery. Be so good, however, to tell us where these bats might be found. Perhaps we can issue a general warning to the public. Carefully worded of course, under the circumstances, carefully worded.”

"Not in London, sir," said Morton. "We have none at the Zoo and the *Desmodontinae* are native to the Americas. I do not believe there are any private local collections. In short, sir, I cannot explain this young woman's bite."

Lestrade's smile dropped. I fancied I could see the rush of thoughts tumbling through his head. A vampire was loose in London. It would take the merest spark to ignite a public frenzy about a real Dracula. An inflamed populace, riots, disturbances perhaps recalling those of the terrible Fenian bombings. The establishment of the London detective force was recent, and the need for it was still being debated in some powerful quarters. Lestrade's authority was, with this one death, of a sudden in jeopardy.

"Now, now, Lestrade'" said Holmes soothingly. I could see he had also been observing our friend's expressions. "I fancy your imagination is running away with you. Let us confine ourselves to the facts as we have them, and I believe we may release our friend Mr. Morton to return to his menagerie."

Morton was only too happy to leave us as Lestrade waved him away. Holmes turned to the detective. "With your permission, I would like to take this keepsake." He held the teeth aloft with an airy wave. "As they have no bearing on the case, I rather think they would make a splendid addition to my own personal Black Museum." He was referring to Scotland Yard's private crime gallery, about which I knew he harboured an intense fascination but had never been permitted to view.

"Take the wretched things," said Lestrade. "But tell me, Mr. Holmes, what do you make of this vampire theory?"

"If those marks are the bite of a vampire bat," said Holmes, pocketing the teeth, "then London does indeed face an unprecedented peril. Good day, Lestrade, we can see ourselves out."

I hurried to keep pace with the striding Holmes. Mercifully the pavements were quieter now, and the elbows and shoulders more contained to their persons. "Did you mean that, Holmes?" I asked him. "Are we indeed facing a dreadful danger?"

"No,' said Holmes simply, "we are not facing any danger."

"But you said …"

"I said, *if* those were the marks of a vampire's teeth. However, those were *not* the marks of a vampire's teeth. Therefore, the peril, being conditional, no longer menaces us. Watson, you are a medical man. Did you closely examine these marks, this bite?"

"Well, no, I did not, but Lestrade had done so, and declared it a bite and then Morton believed …"

"Indeed. Our zoological friend accepted the idea that it was the bite of some animal without applying his own mind to the matter, and he suggested the only beast he could think of with the teeth that would fit the wounds. He was not deducing in a rational sequence, Watson, he was, if I may so express it, working backwards. Reflect: did you observe him studying the bites themselves and analysing them? No? No, indeed. He was carried away with Lestrade's fancy, as perhaps you have been yourself. There is no quicker way of surrendering your powers of deductive reasoning, Watson, than to accept that what you observe is what someone tells you that you observe. Questioning Watson, questioning. It is at the core of all scientific understanding."

I was crestfallen. How many times had Holmes drawn me in and then dismissed me in this way, I wondered to myself. I would almost have taken heart if I could but think I would know better another time, but I knew this hope to be false. I would never know better. Holmes would always trounce me.

"So, we are safe?" I asked him tentatively.

"There is no vampire roaming London, at least, though whether we are ever really safe, I would not hazard to say."

"And the marks?"

"I fear, Watson, that the extreme oddness and yet banality of what caused those marks is what led you astray. Tell me, what is the most common small household injury?"

"Why burns, of course. Stoves, fires, gas lights and still in many homes, candles."

"Indeed. And the lady we observed just now, was she of a slight build?"

"By no means. She was a handsome and well-made woman who would have been stately in life, I feel sure."

"Now I come to a more delicate question. If one were to drop a small ember, perhaps while holding it up in a pair of tongs to light a taper or a gas jet, and it fell into the top of a well-made woman's corset, how would the burn appear?"

I ran through my mind the conditions he had stated, and a moment later exclaimed with wonder, "The ember would lodge in her corset. The burn would appear as two symmetrical spots in the centre of the woman's breast! Good heavens, Holmes! This is extraordinary! It was not a bite at all!"

"No, it was not a bite, and judging from its deep colour, I believe it to have occurred some days since, which perhaps will be confirmed by the pathologist. However, I bethought myself to leave Lestrade a little longer in his somewhat confused garden of thoughts." Holmes reached into his pocket and drew out the false teeth. "This is where my interest lies. I believe these teeth hold the clue to the mysterious death, and perhaps the identity, of that young woman." He strode forward and I hurried in his wake.

When I came into the breakfast room the following morning, I could see at once that Holmes had not been to bed. The air was thick with tobacco smoke, and still in his dress of the previous evening, he reclined over two dining chairs, his feet on the table and the false teeth resting on a short pile of books in front of him.

"Ah, Watson, unable to sleep, I see."

"On the contrary, Holmes, I have slept very soundly for considerably more than eight hours. It is almost nine o'clock in the morning, and I smell the approach of a dish of bacon and some coffee."

I went to the window and throwing back the curtains, flung open the casement. Sunlight streamed in and smoke began to drift out. Holmes roused himself with a dry chuckle as Mrs. Hudson knocked and entered, bearing a generous tray.

"Lord, the smell!" she grumbled. "And I know well where your big boots have been, Mr. Holmes. That's my good tablecloth though how I can call it that now I couldn't honestly say and that's the truth." As she placed the tray on the table, she caught sight of the false teeth. "Oh Lord, give me strength! It's half of someone's head on my best."

Laughing, Holmes scooped the teeth into his pocket. "Just someone's misplaced eating mechanism, Mrs. Hudson. I pity the poor soul who does not keep his own teeth in his head when I see this wondrous spread. Goodness, the best of a pig, and crisp, and is that your own sublime conserve? Mrs. Hudson, I revere you."

She smiled at his charm, no more fooled than I, but warmed nonetheless. “Go on with you, Mr. Holmes, sir. I believe you are the very devil. I will bring some coffee directly.”

I sat at the table and set to, while Holmes cleared away the books and tapped out his noisome pipe. Mrs. Hudson returned to place the coffee on the table and withdrew.

“And what do you make of your keepsake after a night’s study?” I asked him.

“I believe they belong to the woman’s lover and not her murderer, but I believe the two are connected.” He reached behind him to the pile of newspapers stacked upon the footstool and began to rummage through them. “I hope you can clear your afternoon, Watson, as I rather think we are going to observe a game of football.”

My fork paused halfway to my mouth. Holmes had never been known to express the slightest interest in, nor understanding of, sport. “Oh yes?” I said in as offhand a manner as I could summon. “What match shall we see?”

“I rather fancy seeing …” he picked up a folded paper and checked it “Tottenham Hotspur and Liverpool.”

My fork continued its journey and I chewed meditatively. I could ask him why. I could express my surprise or even perhaps frustration at being once again kept in ignorance. I well knew that he was toying with me. Yet my hearty breakfast was suffusing me with a healthy morning warmth and just for the moment I felt equal to this challenge. I would do a little toying of my own.

"What else do you deduce about the teeth, Holmes old man? At what conclusions have you arrived?"

Still oblivious to the hot dish of eggs and bacon, Holmes leant back and tilted the chair in a manner strongly disapproved of by Mrs. Hudson. He held the teeth up in one hand and used the other for explanatory waves and pointing. "They are quite new," he began. "I would say not more than six months old, possibly even less, and expensive. You see they are handmade porcelain and not the more common Waterloo teeth, suggesting that their owner has come into money quite recently. Now observe Watson, it is not a full set for an upper mandible. There are spaces for the owner's remaining strong and healthy teeth. An older man is more likely to require the replacement of every tooth. Thus, I believe we are not looking for an old man, for man it is: the shape of the jawline makes that clear. I believe we are looking for a young man, somewhat concerned with his appearance."

"Fascinating," I said, as I finished my plate and reached for some toast and conserve. "Please go on."

"Now, observe these faint marks on the sides," said Holmes, angling the teeth towards me. "I rather think they may have been caused by one of those new gum shields."

"Ah, the teeth protectors? Gutta-percha I believe? A sound idea for anyone likely to get a knock."

"Yes, yes, indeed. In fact this leads me to believe that we are tracking a sportsman, Watson, and a sportsman either accustomed to some bruising treatment in the pursuit of his game, or perhaps fearing it, and taking care to protect his new investment."

I leant back with satisfaction, my coffee in my hand. "May I summarise? We are in pursuit of a young, vain, sportsman with access to money who has lost his artificial teeth to the death grip of a mysterious corpse."

Mrs. Hudson knocked and entered. "Finished, gentlemen?" She made to clear the table and Holmes let out a short bark.

"My breakfast! What the devil?" He eyed me suspiciously. "Sometimes I almost think, Watson – " but he left his sentence unfinished as I coolly sipped my coffee, my face expressionless.

As we sat in the hansom rattling us towards Crystal Palace later that day, Holmes unfolded part of a newspaper from his greatcoat pocket. "Something is amiss with the Tottenham team, Watson. Read this."

The article described the outcry from fans the previous week when goalkeeper, William Anders, was inexplicably absent on the day of the match. As the team's rising star, his absence was critical, and Tottenham lost the match.

"Oh yes," I said, "I have heard something of this, though as you know, I am more of a rugby man. I believe there were rumours that this chap was being pursued by another club, or something of that nature. Do we expect Anders to be playing today?"

"That remains to be seen. I believe he is listed to play. Altogether I am rather interested in being on the spot."

"Holmes, what does this Anders have to do with the false teeth?"

"If I have deduced aright, I believe he will be missing them."

"They are his teeth?"

"That is my surmise. Recall if you will our proccss of deduction and your admirable summary: young, vain, moneyed sportsman. Anders is all of these."

"But so also are his teammates, surely."

"By no means. These men are amateurs, mostly I understand drawn from the working classes. And I might also add that his teammates have not inexplicably disappeared on the day of an important game, to return without public explanation, nor have they sought the help of Scotland Yard in recent weeks."

"Anders has been to the police?"

"Indeed, he has, but it seems he received no satisfaction from that quarter. His complaint was not held to be serious. He believed his life to be in danger but was reluctant to provide details. Our official friends were justifiably obliged to let the matter rest, indeed believing that successful football players will always attract some animosity from fans of rival teams."

"How on earth do you know this, Holmes?"

"As it happens, I had been following this story in a desultory way and had sought information from Lestrade, who, though willing to provide me with the bare facts, made sure to inform me that this was not 'in my line.' In fact, I believe he was attempting to keep me in my place yesterday by inviting me to the morgue. He prefers that I restrict myself to the eccentric and bizarre, and leave crime to the official force."

"But look here, Holmes, how is it that this Anders has come into money? Perhaps an inheritance?"

"Ah, here we venture into speculation and you know my views about deducing ahead of the data, Watson."

I was a little nettled at his pomposity. "I know that you scorn to speculate as a general rule," I replied, "yet I warrant that I could name half a dozen occasions when you have done just so."

Holmes gazed out the hansom window for a moment, apparently turning this over in his mind. "Very well, Watson, there is perhaps something in what you say, however I grant you only five instances, and in each of those circumstances the surrounding facts were prodigiously suggestive."

I chuckled at his admission. "But not in this case?"

"Not in this case. At present I have four possible explanations to test against the events of the afternoon ahead. Whether these will reduce in number or indeed increase, it is impossible for me to say."

We arrived at the ground a good half hour before the scheduled start of the match. There was a sizeable crowd already in attendance, but it was, I was pleased to see, a peaceful one. To my surprise we made straight for the pavilion, directing our steps to the team changing rooms below ground level.

A harassed looking, sparse-haired man in team colours was remonstrating with a young man in cloth cap and working clothes.

"You should be already kitted up, Sterne! The team is almost ready yonder. Get your kecks on and toss that damned charch!" The young man slouched off with the cigarette still hanging from his lips and his interlocutor turned to us with a momentarily quizzical look. His face lightened. "You'll be Mr Holmes! Most welcome, I'm sure. And Dr. Watson? Good, good, I'm Morrison. Let's us have a little talk before I get this team ready to run out. Still missing a couple," he checked his pocket watch. "But

Howard will be right, and I daresay Lennie with him, so we should be bang up to the elephant."

"And young Anders?" asked Holmes.

"Well, there you have me, in a sense, Mr. Holmes. He is here, but is he here? I mean to say he is in the outer room there with the others but not so bricky. Got the morbs and no mistake. Can't honestly say as he can play but there I am in a pickle. If I put young James back out again this week there will be mafficking in the stands you may be sure, and believe me, we will never take the egg."

I looked enquiringly at Holmes, who nodded to Morrison and said, "So Anders seems preoccupied, but without him playing you will lose."

Morrison looked at him, puzzled. "Yes, so I said just now."

We gained Morrison's permission to speak to Anders and settled ourselves in a small tearoom to the side of the hall. A moment later, Anders came through to join us. He was wiry rather than muscular, of middle height; strong and fit but with a very downcast countenance. A glimpse as he greeted us confirmed Holmes' surmise that the false teeth were indeed his.

"My friend and I know that you are sorely troubled, Mr. Anders," Holmes began. "In fact, I believe you are facing a trial which is beyond your powers to resolve. Mr. Anders, your wife is missing."

He was visibly taken aback for a moment. “She is not my wife, sir.”

“Yes, yes, your common law wife is missing, is she not?”

‘She is, sir, though how you know of this I cannot say.”

“I believe you asked the official police for assistance when your own life was threatened?”

“I did sir.” His voice shook and he rubbed his face with his hand. “They turned me away.”

“Perhaps they were hampered by the fact that they had no names and no evidence.”

“Well how could I give them names?” Anders burst out. “That was the very thing they told me would be punished. Yes, I did ask the police for help, but I had to give it away. God help me, I never thought they would harm Eliza. I got in fair deep with those scoundrels before I knew what they were about. I should never have taken their money and you may be sure I rue it, but it is now all spent, and I thought at least that Eliza was safe. And now they have her, I am sure of it. They are rogues of the worst kind. Mr. Holmes, I don’t know what business you have here but if you are on my side, if there is some power that might aid me, I beg you to act.” He leaned forward with his elbows on his knees, shaking his head in distress.

Holmes inclined gently towards the young man. "Mr. Anders, I have grave news indeed. I regret that I bring you yet more sorrow. Your persecutors did indeed take Eliza, but this much of course you already know, for you were there when she was taken, were you not?"

Anders nodded slowly; his eyes fixed upon Holmes in trepidation.

"I think it may have been an accident, but I am now certain she has been slain."

Anders looked at Holmes in horror, his face a mask of ashen terror. "Killed?" Holmes gave him a slight, sombre nod and the young man put his face in his hands and sobbed.

Morrison was obliged to put young James in the goal after all since the unfortunate Anders was prostrated by shock. He was transported to Scotland Yard where he had the unhappy task of identifying Eliza's body.

Holmes and I sat in thoughtful silence as our cab bore us homeward.

"Well, we missed the game after all," he remarked after some minutes.

I sighed. “That unfortunate young man. Not only this dreadful event but I fancy he might have lost his position on the team.”

“It would certainly be regrettable if that were the case,” remarked Holmes, dusting his legs offhandedly. “It was his position on the team that brought him his troubles.”

“Indeed? How so?”

“Because, Watson, his unique position made him an object of value to the unscrupulous scoundrels who sought to benefit from some dishonest wagering. I think you will find that the expression is ‘fixing.’ They sought to ‘fix’ some matches by influencing our young friend to miss some goals, in effect, to lose deliberately.”

“And this influence was a threat to his life?”

“It became so. Money was first, of course.”

“Hence the teeth.”

“Hence the teeth. However, as they did not receive that which they believed they had purchased, they progressed to threats. But as you saw, while Anders did take his fears to the police, he would not then disclose the information they required to take action, and unfortunately by this stage the money he had accepted was gone. You heard his regrets there. This confirmed for me the sequence of events.

"After Anders' abortive attempt to recruit the protection of the official force, I am certain the miscreants then escalated their threats to include the young woman, Eliza. I believe a plan to kidnap her went awry. Once I heard from Anders' own lips that he had been there when she was abducted, I knew that his silence had been assured by his fears for her safety."

"Abducted!" I said. "Why, that is monstrous! What scoundrels. But how came she to perish?

"You recall that there were no obvious signs of violence upon the corpse? This raised a question in my mind, and I made a point to lean in close to her face. I detected the distinct odour of chloroform. The lack of rigour told us she had died only shortly prior to being brought to the morgue, nonetheless, the odour was surprisingly strong, and I suspected that she had been accidentally murdered by those who had wished to keep her unconscious."

"This is ghastly, Holmes. She was seized from her own home by these criminals who chloroformed her and carried her away!"

"And continued to apply the drug to keep her quiet until they accidentally applied too much. Thereupon they left her at the hospital. Incidentally, that was a most telling detail of Lestrade's. If the young woman had indeed been the victim of some sort of dangerous bite, one would expect her friends to summon a doctor or take her with all speed to the hospital. To leave a body at the service entrance and quit the scene rather suggests a reluctance to be involved with the authorities, which in turn is suggestive of murder rather than injury." He paused thoughtfully for a moment.

"Indeed, it occurs to me, Watson, that we might do well to alter our route and make for Scotland Yard. I rather fancy that Lestrade will be all astonishment at these developments."

I readily assented, and Holmes redirected the driver.

Lestrade welcomed us into his office. Holmes asked him about Anders.

"Well, the young man came in all right," said Lestrade. "And a poor state he was in. Took it quite bad indeed when he saw the young lady. So we know who she is at least, though he could tell us nothing about the bite. That aspect is still a mystery. But Mr Holmes, how in Heaven's name did you figure out he was involved in this?"

"The teeth, Lestrade, the teeth. As you so rightly indicated, they were very much in my line. However, we do have some far graver news to impart, news that is in *your* line."

As Holmes had predicted, Lestrade was indeed all astonishment at the story we had to relate. We took our leave as he bustled off to commence his murder investigation, crying out over his shoulder, "and there is no vampire! Such excellent news!"

We had dismissed the cab, so Holmes and I made our way homeward on foot. I saw with some dismay that the pedestrian throng was dense.

"I say, Holmes," I said, "shall we try some side roads this time? These elbows are too much for me."

"By all means. In fact, I know of a short cut, if you do not object to a rough path."

"Not at all," I replied, and followed him as he ducked down a narrow laneway, wonderfully free of foot traffic. "There is still one thing that puzzles me," I said to his back, as there was no room to walk abreast. "How came Anders' teeth to be in the young lady's hand?"

"Ah, well. I think it would help if you visualise the scene." Holmes took a turn into another anonymous lane. "The young couple was preparing to retire, hence her state of deshabille, when the rogues broke in. They restrained young Anders and seized the young lady, immediately holding the chloroform to her face. In the moments before she succumbed to unconsciousness, in her panic she reached out and grabbed whatever came within her reach."

"It was the teeth!" I cried. "I can see it. They lay on the bedside table."

"So I believe," said Holmes. "And they remained in her grasp until she died. It was fortunate indeed that Lestrade thought to bring me in on what he believed would be a little joke at my expense. If he had not done so, perhaps London would be shut in to save the populace from a giant vampire bat." He chuckled.

“Well now, Watson,” he said, as we emerged miraculously through a narrow gap between two houses into Baker Street. “What do you think of my little shortcut? Rather in my line, wouldn’t you say?”

# The Case of the Journalist's Stepmother

## The Case of the Journalist's Stepmother

"I say, Holmes," I said, as we made our way along the busy footpath, "what do you think about this new clairvoyant everyone is talking about?" A few strides further along, when he did not answer, I glanced across at my companion and saw that he was in his altered musical state, eyes on the distance, head gently swaying in time to his internal recital. We had just come from a concert at Covent Garden where the Shinner Quartet had played Bach's double concerto, and I could see that Holmes was replaying in his mind the magnificent music. "Holmes? What do you think?"

"I think, Watson, that the second of the concertos for two violins evokes more of the pathos intended by the composer than the first, yet the structure somehow implies a cooler state. We have observed a lady violinist playing with an almost masculine intellect. Most instructive."

"Holmes, you simply do not listen to me." I strode forward as Holmes paused, causing other pedestrians to grumble as they made their way around him.

"Watson, I beg your forgiveness. I confess I am never quite prepared for the moment after a concert when my uplifted state introduces me once again to the pavement." He sighed. "It was sublime, and it is over. Now, what was it you were asking me?"

I felt a little remorse to have broken into his rhapsodic reverie for something trivial, but so it was. "This medium, as she styles herself, Madam Liliana." I said. "Have you been reading the reports in the paper?"

"Certainly. You know I like to follow the more outré of the stories we, the reading public, are so very privileged to be served." I winced a little at his sarcasm, as I well knew Holmes' views of my occasionally penning an account of one of his cases for publication.

"Well, what do you think?"

"Watson, you know well that I don't think in advance of the data. I absorb. I file. I retain."

"But all these reports of late, of séances and mediums communing with the dead – do you believe in the occult?"

"Naturally I do."

"You do?" It was my turn to stop and cause a disruption to the flow of pedestrian traffic. I received some sharp nudges from grumbling strangers, and quickly moved on to keep pace with Holmes. "You believe in the occult, Holmes?"

"Watson, Watson," he chuckled, "and you a medical man. If I did not believe in that which cannot be seen, I would indeed have a difficult time of it in my unique line of work. However, if you mean do I believe in the supernatural, most decidedly I do not. I am firmly with the corporeal. I believe in charlatans, and I believe in crooks, and I believe in victims. These I can see. For these there is evidence."

Chastened, for of course I was not thinking of the word in its medical sense, I continued walking at his side in silence. As we reached the street door of our lodgings, Holmes turned to me. "Watson, I believe you have acquaintances at that newspaper of yours. If you really wish to do a service to the susceptible, which I have always understood to be the case, I suggest you invite a sensible journalist to meet with me here so I can set out for him in detail how charlatans and fraudsters can be detected and their shameless trickery exposed." He stepped through the door and firmly took the stairs up to the drawing room.

I stood on the pavement, for the moment stunned. Holmes would speak to a journalist! I was all astonishment, and I hastily followed him up.

The journalist I thought to approach was young Gabriel Tobias. He had been at the paper for something less than a twelvemonth but had shown by a steady application to be earnest and less inclined to be carried away by the extraordinary or the vulgar than many of his brethren had shown themselves to be. I had no official standing at the paper, of course. I merely met on occasion with the editor and submitted an account of a case of Holmes' as the opportunity presented. I called on the editor in his offices and put before him the proposal. As I had anticipated, he was delighted and almost rubbed his hands with pleasure. He endorsed my thinking that Tobias would make an admirable envoy and sent for the young man immediately.

Gabriel Tobias approached the glass door to the editor's office and tentatively knocked.

"Looking for me, sir?" he said as he entered the room. I observed a young man of middle height, rather stocky than otherwise and wearing neat, reddish side-whiskers. He was quietly spoken with a serious demeanour, and altogether I congratulated myself on my plan. Here indeed was Holmes' "sensible" young man.

My friend the editor explained the commission and I keenly watched the young journalist's face, anticipating his eager response. I confess I was a little disappointed to see that Tobias remained expressionless, for Holmes' name was well known at the paper. I glanced at the editor, who appeared to find nothing amiss, and decided that imperturbability is a demonstration of good sense. Tobias and I immediately set off together to Baker Street.

Holmes was at his most genial, even taking his role as host so seriously that he ordered tea. We sat at the table as Mrs. Hudson settled the tray and placed the pot, cups and, I was pleased to see, a plate of scones about us before quitting the room. Young men are famously hungry and I expected to see Tobias eye the scones keenly, but again, the imperturbability. He merely took out his notepad and looked expectantly at Holmes, who poured the tea.

Holmes began. “I had planned to commence by listing for you the most common of the frauds perpetrated by those everyday villains purporting to communicate with the so-called afterlife. However now that you are here, Mr. Tobias, I feel far more inclined to begin with a question.”

“Certainly sir,” said Tobias. “Please do so.” He poised his pencil, eyes on Holmes.

“Mr. Tobias, or whatever your name really is, why are you impersonating a journalist?”

Tobias and I both leapt to our feet. I spluttered my outrage, but I saw that Tobias’s face registered fear, not anger. Holmes, meanwhile, merely reached for a scone, a slow smile across his face.

“Please don’t distress yourself,” he said. “Perhaps I was a little unthinking. Watson will tell you that it would not be the first time I have been so. I shall make myself a little clearer: I have no doubt that you are a journalist, but I know that you are not Gabriel Tobias.”

I was flabbergasted. I had read this young man’s pieces in the paper over the past few months and had indeed collected him from the newspaper's own offices with the blessings of his editor. He *was* Gabriel Tobias.

The young man, still standing, lifted his head with dignity. "I am not. However, I am not impersonating Gabriel Tobias. He is my own invention and all his work has been my own. My name is Oldham, Lucinda Oldham, and yes, I am a woman." Here she slowly peeled off one of her side-whiskers and removed her bulky waistcoat, revealing a slighter and more feminine outline. "I am not to blame for the deception, Mr Holmes. I have skills that I wish to exercise and my family benefits from my position materially. However, I am not permitted to do an honest day's work under my real name and in my real identity. Hence the subterfuge. I repeat, the deception is not of my making."

Her indignant expression faded and she again took her seat, as did I. "May I ask you something, Mr. Holmes?" she said. "I have encountered no difficulty amongst my male colleagues in sustaining this disguise for many months now. I am satisfied that I am not guilty of complaisance in this matter, yet your discovery of my secret appears to have been immediate. Would you do me the kindness of favouring me with an explanation?"

Holmes placed his palms together beneath his chin.

"Details, Miss Oldham, details; suggestive in themselves, persuasive in their accumulation. A hand more delicately boned than a bulky frame is not conclusive. Nor is a gentle voice, nor is the absence of evidence of tobacco use – ash, stains, smell - in a journalist, and yet you will allow that your brethren are, as a class, notorious smokers. But when I see a well-whiskered young man with a curiously smooth upper lip, who barely glances at an entire plate of scones, I feel myself to be in possession of enough indicative facts to draw a likely conclusion."

Miss Oldham bowed her head in something between acknowledgement and disappointment, then raised it again to look directly at Holmes.

"Mr. Holmes, it is now within your power to undo this deceit, but if my plea carries any weight with you, I beg you not to do so."

I was transfixed by the young person before me. She sat in quiet confidence, awaiting a response from Holmes. I looked to him, as he set down the cup from which he had been calmly drinking.

"I have no personal wish to interfere with your career," he said, and I found myself sighing with relief. "However, I propose some terms. If you agree to them, you have my silence on this matter, as I am quite sure you already have Watson's." At this of course I nodded.

"My terms are thus: you will write an article according to my wishes and you will use the facts I will provide for you. Your article will demonstrate that everything is explained by the physical and science tells us what is natural: there is no supernatural."

The young woman was evidently thinking through the implications of Holmes' proposal. I watched her in some consternation: I believed that Holmes had rather overstepped the mark, and that she would become distressed. I was surprised therefore to see a faint trace of amusement on her still pallid face.

“You put me in something of an unusual position, Mr. Holmes. I consider myself to be a woman of science and would readily accede to your request were it not for the fact that a member of my own family earns a living practising in this field. It has frequently caused me much concern, and indeed embarrassment, but my stepmother believes herself to be a medium between this life and the next. I fear that it would be distressing to her if I were to write an article denouncing such claims.”

“She knows of your newspaper work and your alias, then?”

“Well, as it happens, no, she does not. She expresses decidedly firm and traditional views about a woman’s role, Mr. Holmes, which do not coincide with mine. In fact my sister and I have established our own separate home, leaving my father and stepmother, because we came to believe that peace for my father would be most readily realised in this way.” I perceived a faint cloud cross her brow, and it was clear that this young woman held great affection for her father and was pained by some darkness concerning him. “Perhaps you are right,” she said after a moment’s reflection. “If my stepmother does not know that this expose is written by me, then I cannot be held to account for it.” At this she laughed, and for the first time I saw the young girl beneath the sober, adopted character. “I see that more subterfuge is in store for me,” she said. “Well, let me agree to this challenge:

I accept your terms, Mr. Holmes." At this, she took up her notebook and pencil, ready to begin.

"One moment," I said. "I am all curiosity about your stepmother's claims. How does her power evidence itself? Does she hold séances? Do people apply to her to speak with their dead relatives?"

"Dr. Watson, she holds meetings, which my sister and I have never been permitted to attend." She turned to Holmes. "My sister, Adelaide, holds very much my own views in all things." She went on, "Unfortunately I cannot tell you what transpires at these meetings, however I can tell you that every Thursday evening at least four or five strangers come to the house, the parlour door is shut, and curious noises disturb our evening for the better part of two hours. Perhaps I should say, used to disturb us, since now Adelaide and I enjoy the freedom of an independent home."

"You fascinate me," said Holmes, leaning forward. His remark surprised me, since I knew that Holmes had more than once exposed such charlatans and disabused their unfortunate gulls. He well knew the type of performance engaged in and many a time had I heard his tirades concerning the evils of Madam Blavatsky and her ilk. However, in a moment it was clear that his fascination related to something else that Tobias, or rather Miss Oldham, had said. "You have always been prevented from attending these meetings. Most informative. And when did your father marry – I beg your pardon, your stepmother's name?"

"My stepmother, the second Mrs. Oldham, chooses to use the rather colourful alias of Liliana Krawzenko."

"Good heavens!" I said. "Madam Liliana! Why that's the very one I was reading about." I rose hastily and went to the window seat, rummaging through an untidy pile of newspapers. "Ah!" I exclaimed. "Here it is," and I held aloft the Borderland Journal of a few days since. But before I could find and read out the short piece concerning local spiritualists, Miss Oldham interrupted.

"Yes, I am aware of the article, Dr. Watson. It was not, as you see, written by me, and of course not carried by the paper with which I am connected. I believe my stepmother was rather pleased with it than otherwise, providing as it does some measure of endorsement of her enterprises. You see my father called upon Adelaide and me that same evening. We could plainly see that something was troubling him, though he would not share his burden with us. He did however say that my stepmother, whom he calls Lilly, was planning a larger than usual meeting this week as a consequence of the article. I believed him to be unhappy about this, but he did not say so. I found after he had left that Adelaide shared my view of the circumstances."

Holmes looked thoughtful, and I placed the paper back on the pile. "I wonder..." he said musingly. We waited patiently for him to form his thought into words. "Today is Wednesday," he said finally. "The meeting will be tomorrow night."

"Yes, that is so."

"And your stepmother knows nothing about your masculine alias?"

"She does not."

"I am willing to wager that she will not recognise you as Gabriel Tobias, nor me as, shall we say, your recently widowed uncle. What say you?"

Before Miss Oldham could reply, I broke in. "And I?"

"No, Watson, I fear not. I fancy three of us participating in Madam's performance would risk exposure."

Disappointed though I was, I agreed. I rang for the Boots and dispatched him to the telegraph office with a message requesting admittance to Madam Liliana's mysterious soiree the following evening.

As Holmes and I sat over coffee next morning, we heard a sharp rap at the street door followed by hurried steps up to the breakfast room. The Boots failed to precede two young women, who almost tumbled into the room in their haste. As he called out "the Misses Oldham," the women spoke simultaneously. I confess I must have gaped at them, with my cup halfway to my lips, as I attempted to make out what it was they were trying to communicate.

“Ladies, ladies,” said Holmes calmly, as he rose and offered them chairs. He waved away the Boots who still stood at the door, indecisive. Holmes turned to Lucinda. “Miss Oldham,” he said, “clearly something has transpired since we spoke yesterday. I take it this is your sister, the elder Miss Oldham?”

Introductions were made and we all took our seats.

The young women, alike in complexion and colouring but differing in both height and air, Miss Adelaide being the taller and more confident, shared an opaque glance. Lucinda nodded to Adelaide, who began to speak.

“You must know, Mr. Holmes, that I have for some time been harbouring a secret from my sister.” Again, they exchanged a look that I could not interpret. “When Lucy came home last night and told me of the adventure planned with you for tonight, I was in some considerable consternation, and finally came to the decision that I must tell her everything.”

“Pray continue,” said Holmes.

Miss Oldham adjusted the buttons at her wrists and took a deep breath. “I believe that my father’s wife was responsible for my mother’s death.”

“No, Adelaide,” cried Miss Lucinda. “I tell you it is not possible. Our mother died of a weak heart.” She turned to Holmes. “It has always been understood in our family, Mr. Holmes. My mother was an invalid and died of her condition when I was still an infant."

"Lucinda, you know I have cared for you since that time and would not distress you for the world, but I know I am right." Miss Oldham now appealed to Holmes. "I was nine years old yet I can remember these events as though they happened two days since. My mother was upstairs in her room, in bed as usual. I had recently been in to see her, to bring her the baby." She nodded towards Lucinda. "My mother loved to see the baby." She paused a moment, as though collecting herself from some great and private grief. "She would hold the baby in her arms when she was feeling strong, but at times she was entirely enervated by her illness and I would hold the baby to her face for her to kiss. On this day, my mother had seemed cheerful, but weak. As I was carrying the baby back to the nurse, I saw that my father was greeting a visitor in the hall below. It was a woman I had never seen before, though I have come to know her well in the years since. It was Madame Krawzenko, of that I am certain. At that moment the nurse called to me, and I went to the nursery but I could hear that my father and the visitor mounted the stairs and entered my mother's room. My father then quitted the room and shut the door, leaving the two women alone.

"A short time later I was amusing myself in the garden, as I was accustomed to doing, when there was a sudden uproar in the house. Steps and shouting, and the banging of doors. I saw the parlourmaid run out through the front gates still in her apron. I learnt later she was going to fetch the doctor but sadly her endeavour was in vain. My mother had died. Mr. Holmes, my mother had died in her bed when that woman was alone with her."

"Even if this were so, it does not mean Madam murdered her. You have said yourself that your mother was an invalid."

"Mr. Holmes, please do not take Lucy to visit that woman in this secretive way. I know what she has done and I do not want my sister in contact with her. In fact this was the real object behind our removal from my father's home. I am sure you can imagine that is not easy for two young women, even of an independent nature, to find the resources to run a household, be it ever so modest, as is ours. This is why my younger sister, whom I should be protecting, goes into the world masquerading as a man. The fact that we are living unchaperoned materially diminishes our future prospects, but I believed we had no choice."

Holmes sipped his coffee, surely now cold, and carefully replaced the cup in the saucer.

"I have no wish to come between two sisters. Perhaps we can agree on a compromise. Would you consent to my taking Watson with me?"

I felt a thrill of anticipation as I watched the two young women exchange a long and thoughtful look. They appeared to be conversing in silence, understanding one another without words. Miss Lucinda gave a small nod and they both turned to Holmes.

"Yes," said Miss Oldham. "We agree."

Just as the young women had left for home, we received a reply from Madam Liliana: she regretted that the company for her Thursday soiree was now complete, however she was pleased to offer us a private interview the following evening. She named her terms. I gave a low whistle. “That’s steep,” I said.

“Apparently the invisible telegraphs to the netherworld do not come cheaply. However in the name of science let us accept.”

We had settled between us that Holmes would adopt the character of Mr. Spencer, a gentleman seeking communication with a childhood friend, Sophie Oldham ne Morse. This was of course the young women’s mother. A shabby astrakhan coat, a pair of thick pince-nez, a thin beard and a cane transformed Holmes into a nervous and uncertain gentleman. I was to assume the role of the silent companion and need only put on my own coat. We set off on foot for our appointment.

I had read of séances and seen reports of purported encounters with the dead. I expected a shadowy room, thick velvet hangings and a mysteriously veiled figure. However, a neat maid showed us into the parlour, and I was surprised to find myself in a bright, modern room well-lit by gas and a low fire. Madam Liliana welcomed us and bade us sit at a small covered table. She was well, if a little flamboyantly, dressed, almost matronly in aspect but with an unusual, almost severe gaze.

Seating herself at the opposite side of the table, she said in a low, rich voice, "Who brings you here, Mr. Spencer? What voice from beyond is calling to you?"

Holmes shifted uncomfortably and looked toward me, through his thick glasses, as though seeking my help. The feebleness of his character was most convincing. "Go on, old man," I said gently to him. "You must speak."

He glanced at Madam Liliana and away, folding and unfolding his hands. "Sophie Morse," he said softly. "Late of Camberwell, and dead these twelve years."

At this name, Madam Liliana froze, her hard eyes unblinking. "Sophie Morse," she said slowly. "Sophie Morse." After a moment she appeared to recover herself and a strange brightness came into her stern eye. She gave a slight nod. She closed her eyes and placed her hands on the table in front of her. "Sophie Morse, are you there?" There was silence for several moments. "Sophie, Sophie! Speak!" I could feel an almost imperceptible throbbing in the room. The ruddy flickering of the fire suddenly flared to brightness. Madam Liliana threw her head back and cried, "She is here!"

Abruptly the gas was extinguished, and we were thrown into near darkness but for the firelight. Madam Liliana's head dropped forward and I felt a strange vibration through the floor. She rolled her head from side to side, uttering a low moan. "No," she said in a rough, choking voice, "no! Leave me in peace."

Then she began mumbling. "The child," I heard her say. "The child. Save. Oh. Child." She tossed her head, crying out. "Child. Help!"

My heart palpitated at this strange and alarming scene. Clearly the woman was in anguish, calling out for a child to be saved from a harm only she could perceive. I was on the point of rising to render what assistance I could, but as though reading my mind, Holmes reached out and gripped my arm.

We watched the woman's face, fascinated, as the calls became more urgent. "Save me from the child! No! I can't breathe! Bolster, eiderdown! Oh, can't breathe, feathers! It's the child! It's the child! Help me."

The neat maid showed us out barely ten minutes later. I was still profoundly troubled by what we had witnessed and said as much to Holmes as we made our way down the front steps. Holmes folded the pince-nez into the inner pocket of his coat.

"What, the lights went out? The floor vibrated? Watson, this is decidedly not evidence of the supernatural. I do not need to crawl under her table to see that there is a rudimentary system of buttons on the floor Madam can press with her foot."

"But the trance, Holmes. She was in a trance."

"Was she indeed? And you have been to the theatre, I believe, Watson. You are familiar with the concept of people pretending to be other than they are. Indeed, look at our young friend Miss Lucinda, who every day goes to work in the character of a man, a competent, capable man at that, and has no trouble convincing those near to her. As I recall, you were somewhat surprised at that revelation."

"And yet how do you explain what this woman said? She knew something, she knew that a child was responsible for the death of the young ladies' mother. Now if only we can figure out who this evil child was."

"Watson, plainly the child was the nine-year-old Adelaide. And how do I explain what she said? You know my methods: I explain it by excluding the impossible and examining that which remains. In this case, since it is impossible for dead people to speak at all, let alone through the living, the woman is either lying or delusional. If she is lying, we must needs discover the reason. If she is deluded, there we will leave the matter as of no interest."

He stalked ahead, as though the conversation were complete.

I hurried up to him. "But look here, Holmes, we can communicate by telegraph, and we can't see that. Why should there not be other means of communicating yet to be understood?"

"Because Watson, the telegraph operates in waves that can be measured. Our romantically aliased friend operates in ways that cannot be measured. Therefore, she is a fraud or she is a lunatic.

I lean toward the former, but whether she truly believes the child murdered her own mother or whether she is making mischief on a quite extraordinary scale, we have yet to establish. And you will have noticed that her trance did not leave her too distressed to accept her rather extravagant fee."

We had arrived at the young ladies' home. Miss Lucinda opened the door to us, her face clearly showing a lively anticipation to hear what we would relate but her actions those of a demure young lady. "Please come through, Mr. Holmes, Dr. Watson. Adelaide is in the drawing room and Father is here also, as you requested."

She showed us into a pleasant and feminine room, comfortable though small. Miss Adelaide came forward to meet us in some agitation, and introduced us to her father.

Mr. Oldham was a dignified man but distracted and unsettled. Before we could begin, he said, "Mr. Holmes, my daughters mean the world to me."

At this, Adelaide fussed us into taking a seat on the settee while she and her sister took the armchairs and her father stood by the window.

"Your feelings for your daughters are not in question, sir," said Holmes. "As you are aware, Watson and I have come from an appointment with your wife. I confess that we were obliged to enact a little deception to gain our end, hence my garb, and in fact I would wish the tale we now have to tell were not so grave."

Thereupon Holmes related to them what we had witnessed, and the ghastly accusations made by Madam Liliana. His story was greeted with a deathly silence. Miss Lucinda's face was a horrified white. She gripped the arms of the chair rigidly. Miss Adelaide's expression was one of outrage. She looked to her father in a fury.

"You see?" she said. "That woman deals in death! You know she brought death to my mother and now she is trying to bring it to me!"

Her father stepped forward to sit on the edge of a chair by the hearth. I could see that he was overcome with powerful emotions and a single, dry sob choked him before he managed to compose himself.

Holmes allowed the intensity within this small room to gather for another moment before he calmly said, "I have asked myself why Madam Liliana would lie in this way; why she would implicate a child of nine in a murder."

Miss Adelaide looked at him penetratingly. "Because, Mr. Holmes, her currency is death. Death is where she lives and it is all she understands. She killed my mother."

Mr Oldham spoke, his voice uncertain and his head held low. "That is not so."

"I think we can take it that someone hastened her end," said Holmes. "Yesterday I managed to track down the doctor's report.

Scant though it may be, it is clear that she was expected to live a good many months. Thus, my question to you, Mr. Oldham, is how can you be certain that Madam Liliana was not responsible?"

Mr. Oldham groaned. "Give me strength," he muttered to himself. Then lifting his head, he said clearly, "Because, God forgive me, it was I." There was not a sound in the room. The young women froze, unable even to exchange a glance. Mr. Oldham went on, "Bitter, bitter unhappy day. I acquiesced to my dear wife's fervent wishes and I have never ceased to regret that I did so. Melancholy has saturated my being since that day. I live for my daughters, yet how have I served them? By welcoming evil into their home. My own craven wish to silence that which I feared might bring my destruction has driven my dear children from my hearth. And now you bring me the dreadful information that that woman, this night, has attempted to blacken the name of my own child. To what end I do not know, but you may be sure there is deep malice here and it will not go unanswered." He paused, and gave a low moan. "My action was one of loving kindness but what did it profit me these many years?" At this, the young women came to him and sat at his feet caressing him, with tears on their cheeks and loving murmurs on their lips.

He told us the painful tale: The girls' mother, gravely ill and suffering unremitting pain, begged him for her release. With the greatest unwillingness, he agreed, but on condition that she promise to speak to him from beyond the grave, that she bring her soul to bear with every effort to reach him. Thus they made a pact. Madam Liliana was summoned that day so the women could make what arrangements for communicating between the worlds that they might. And thus, also, Madam Liliana became party to the couple's dreadful secret. A wicked woman, she chose to hold this threat over Mr. Oldham, and wishing the respectability of marriage and a family home as a measure of protection for her questionable occupation, she entered his home as the girls' stepmother. Then, as workmen came to make secret changes beneath the floors and behind the walls, the truth came home to him: she was an unashamed fraud, a swindler whose prey was the sorrowing and bereft. She had tricked his dead wife as she had now tricked him.

His daughters were overcome with feeling. Holmes and I made to leave the small family to their tearful reconciliation, but Miss Lucinda rose and saw us to the front door.

"I will write the article Mr. Holmes. I am quite determined to expose that charlatan and her shameful practices." She turned back towards the drawing room. "I am grateful that my sister and I are now in full possession of the dreadful facts, for I know we can bring solace to our father and strength for what must be done. May I call upon you tomorrow morning? I believe I have much to learn from your experiences and I hope you will find me a ready pupil."

Holmes agreed and they made their arrangements. As we strolled home through the thinning evening crowds, Holmes was meditative, swinging his cane and looking thoughtfully down at the pavement. "You believed that Madam Liliana was actually speaking the dead woman's words, did you not Watson?" he asked.

"Well I, that is to say … bless me, Holmes, she was so dashed convincing."

"Was she, Watson? Why did I not experience her performance – for that is what it was – in the same way?"

I believed him to be ruminating and not actually asking for my reply so I said nothing as we turned into Baker Street.

"I cannot help but wonder why, Watson. We are privileged to be living in this age of science. Our certainty about the world expands rapidly, every day new understandings eclipse the old. Why, then, are people so foolish as to seek for something other, something that obfuscates and confuses? The 'subliminal uprush,' the 'supermundane,' the, I believe I have this right, 'phantasmogenetic.' Huh!" Holmes was scornful. "It is almost as though they fear that which is clear and measurable to find comfort in the obscure and mysterious." Holmes sighed as we opened the street door. "Watson, I know I am of this tribe, but in all truth, I feel myself alien to it."

As I followed Holmes up the stairs, I replied thoughtfully. "Indeed Holmes, there is nothing of the spiritual about you. If it cannot be measured, you do not appreciate it." I paused for a moment. "Oh, and by the way, I believe the Shinner Quartet is playing at the Crystal Palace tomorrow night. I had thought you might like to attend with me – ah, but of course, a concerto cannot be scientifically measured, and is therefore to be disdained. I shall have to go alone."

Holmes stopped at the top of the stairs and laughed out loud. "Touché, Watson, old man, touché. You have in one stroke brought me back to being human. I wouldn't miss the concert for the world: Let us be sure to get tickets in the morning."

# The Case of the Anonymous Letter

## The Case of the Anonymous Letter

"Holmes, this really is too much!" I eyed the broken glass pieces of my uncle's photographic plate in my hands. "That was the only Daguerreotype of my aunt that I had. Why the deuce you wanted to break it …"

"My dear Watson, I did not *want* to break it. I merely used it as a counterweight to this pocket watch. The glass plate, you understand, was just one and a half times the mass of the watch and my experiment …"

"Your experiment be damned!" I burst out. I lurched to the door – my old leg injury had been giving me merry hell – and flicked my hat from the rack onto my head and left, unshaven, unbreakfasted and unsettled as I was.

My aunt Helena had recently died, and I was still in mourning, for though only my aunt, we had been very close. My mother, her sister, had died when I was four years old and Aunt Helena had stepped in as my new mother without hesitation and with a full and loving heart. The senseless loss of the photographic plate upset rather than angered me.

A brisk, though rather lopsided walk through a chilly Covent Garden, up Tottenham Court Road and around through Piccadilly brought me back to Baker Street in a more pacified and philosophical frame of mind. I found Mrs. Hudson in what appeared to be an altercation with Holmes, who was standing in the parlour, a pistol in one hand and the coal scuttle in the other, his smoking jacket swinging open on his soiled and tie-less dinner shirt and trousers.

"I will not, Mr. Holmes, sir, I will not. Dr. Watson will tell you the very same. Oh Dr. Watson, here you are and can tell him, do. Tell Mr. Holmes, sir, tell him that I cannot abide the gun shots and the explosions another moment. They shatter my very nerves. Not to mention the neighbours, sir. I can scarce put my nose out of the front door but one or another of them bustles over with the 'whatever has the gentleman been a-doing of now, Elsie? Is he a-murdering of one of them clients of his?' "

I was momentarily taken aback to learn that Mrs. Hudson, long-suffering, ever present, imperturbable Mrs. Hudson, was called Elsie. But I quickly rallied to take the matter in hand.

"Mrs. Hudson, perhaps I can help. I think Holmes has been under a very particular strain of late. Perhaps he needs a little rest now that the recent case, and such a nasty business, is resolved. Perhaps I can persuade him to take a day or two at the seaside."

"Perhaps?" snarled Holmes, dropping the scuttle with a clatter. "Perhaps? *Perhaps* I need a *case*, Watson! And failing that, perhaps I need a little medical assistance to see me through this utterly dreary and interminable life." He slumped and turned to the low fire, gently placing the pistol alongside the Persian slipper. He placed both hands on the mantelpiece and slowly lowered his head until his brow rested on the edge between his hands. "Watson", he said. "Watson, I believe I am at my wits' end."

Mrs. Hudson slowly turned her head to me, her angry eyes now softened to a look of almost maternal care. I returned her look.

"My dear Holmes." I stepped towards him. He was immobile, forehead still resting on the mantelpiece. "Holmes, old chap. Come now. How about some oysters and a chop at Giorgio's and then we can see what's on at Covent Garden?" I turned to the stilled Mrs. Hudson and waved my hand hurriedly. "Mrs. Hudson, quick! There's the Evening Standard. See whether you can find a concert somewhere, a recital perhaps."

Holmes slowly raised his head with a distant gleam in his eye. "Ah, but better than Giorgio's and a concert – I believe I can hear a carriage at the street door." He snapped around, his hands instantly mobile. "Mrs. Hudson, I trust that execrable Boots has retained at least some of his buttons. I believe he is about to show in a new client."

And so it proved. After Mrs. Hudson had hurried out, we heard a quick yelp then the scramble of the Boots descending the stairs at a multiple, followed by a more sedate and accompanied return. Mrs. Hudson herself knocked and stepped into the room. “Miss Catherine Sully, sir,” she said and made way as a rather striking young woman swept in; Holmes, instantly suave and accommodating, introducing us and ushering her to the basket chair.

“I see you made an early start, in spite of the difficulties with the dogs.”

“Oh, those dogs! But you know how …” Her hand flew to her cheek. “Good heavens, Mr. Holmes! He has told you I was coming!”

But before Holmes could make his customary explanation, there was a second knock at the street door. I caught a moment of surprise in Holmes’ eyes. Clearly, he had not anticipated the complication of a duplicate circumstance. A moment later we heard the very hesitant knock of an uncertain Mrs. Hudson at the door. “Yes,” called Holmes.

Mrs. Hudson cautiously peered around the door’s edge, long-schooled to stay away when clients were in, equally well-indoctrinated never to let slip a new case.

“I’m sorry Mr. Holmes, sir, only there’s a gentleman as says it’s most urgent and pressing and wouldn’t take no for an answer.”

But before Holmes could reply, and to the great surprise of the young lady, a young gentleman burst past Mrs. Hudson into the room. His frantic look swept from Holmes to me to Holmes, then stopped at the young lady. If anything, his dishevelled look became yet more tousled.

"Catherine?" he gasped. "Catherine, here?" then he looked at Holmes, at me, at the young lady and finally at Mrs. Hudson, who, with the wisdom of long experience gently backed through the door and closed it with a quiet snick.

The young woman stood hastily, clasping her reticule in front of her. She glanced swiftly at the young man, then back at Holmes. "This is my brother," she said, but at the same moment the young man burst out with "This is my fiancée, sir."

Later, after a cup of tea, chairs positioned to the fire, Holmes at his most urbane, and my own inane gabbling about the 'unseasonable' fogs we had been experiencing, (unseasonable? Fogs in a London January?) we had brought the room back from its hectic moment to something considerable calmer.

Holmes had remained standing and placed himself on the hearth with his back to the fire and one long finger gently touching his forehead.

"So, as I understand it, you, Miss Sully, claim that this gentleman is Mr. Ronald Wentworth, your brother." The young lady held her teacup still and nodded. Holmes spun slightly on his heel and addressed the young gentleman, who hastily placed his cup on the tea table. "And you, sir, claim that you are Mr. Ralph Benniston, this young lady's affianced." The young man nodded owlishly.

Holmes turned to me. "Well, Watson, I propose we follow your plan – oysters and a chop at Giorgio's and then a concert at Covent Garden. We shall lock these two youngsters in this room and I imagine that by the time we return, after perhaps a little visit to Flamingos on the way home – their cognac really is excellent – they will have settled their most curious differences and be ready with a united story for us."

The two young people exchanged a swift look, at first wide eyed with concern, then imperceptibly relaxing into what looked to my jaded eyes like a deeply familiar humour. The young lady had the good grace to blush, the young man to sink his eyes and clear his throat.

We did not need to have recourse to a long evening of diversions to arrive at a coherent story. The young couple were neither siblings nor were they betrothed. They were, however, what they referred to as 'in love,' at which Holmes flicked his facc to the side and tchd, "yes, yes," impatiently.

Their story was an odd one. Catherine, it seemed, was the orphan daughter of a mother who recently died in a French sanatorium and a civilian father who died in India during a temporary period of administrative service when Catherine was a baby. She had lived with her mother in Cornwall until recently: a retired life but a relatively comfortable one. Soon after her mother, a chronic consumptive, removed to France, Catherine received an anonymous letter containing a most sinister accusation: that she was in reality the illegitimate daughter of a well-known and wealthy mill owner, Mr. Arthur Benniston. At this name, I stirred, and shifted my gaze from Miss Sully's face to that of the young man's. He gave an almost imperceptible twitch. I glanced at Holmes, whose gaze had sharpened like a cat's.

"You will understand my anger at this claim against my parent's honour," said Catherine. "I immediately determined to travel to France at once to place the letter before my mother and ask her what it could mean, and who would wish to cause us harm. However, fortune was against me and I arrived at the sanatorium just hours too late. My mother had experienced an unexpected relapse and died overnight. The nuns were very kind to me. They showed me to the small chapel where my mother lay, ghostly pale in death but, I was comforted to see, peaceful. They had arranged the funeral for two days hence. I own I was distressed, and the nuns gently showed me my mother's room. It was a small, cell-like space with a crucifix above a narrow, leaded window, a modest cot covered with a thin white counterpane and a small chest of drawers covered in faded fabric.

"The nuns brought me some coffee and rolls – I had not yet breakfasted - and at my request left me alone in my mother's room. I hoped to find some solace in her familiar prayer book, which I found readily enough in the top drawer, resting on a clean but rather coarse nightgown identical to the one in which she was now laid out. I lifted the nightgown out of the drawer and shook it open. It seemed diminutive as I held it against myself. It was not just grief I felt at that moment, gentlemen," said Catherine earnestly. "The grief was blent with guilt and, I am afraid, curiosity. Guilt for not accompanying my mother on what transpired to be her last trip; curiosity about what she might have been able to tell me concerning the anonymous letter.

"I know you must consider me a heartless daughter, Mr. Holmes, Dr. Watson. In truth I believe I am. But you did not know my mother. She was a very private woman and unbent so very little even to me, and even when I was a very small child, that I have long believed myself unloved." She stole a glance at young Benniston, who was leaning forward with his elbows on his knees, circling the rim of his hat through his hands.

Holmes' gaze took in the tableau for a moment before he said, "Miss Sully, I make no surmise about the quality of what you refer to as your heart, and neither does it interest me." I saw both the young people start at Holmes' curt words. I leaned forward to reassure them but before I could speak Holmes snapped, "Watson here will tell you that I am a bear, Miss Sully. Bear I may be, and indeed you will find I do not waste time on sentiment, however I am of the view that you did not call upon me to join you in maudlin reflections about your bereavement. Pray continue your story."

Miss Sully collected herself and took up her tale.

"As I held the small nightgown against myself on the morning of my mother's death, a slip of paper fluttered to the floor, apparently falling from within the folds of the gown. I bent to pick it up, thinking it was perhaps laundry instructions, and found that it was a list of French words and their English translations."

At this I detected a quiver of irritation pass through Holmes. "An English woman in France has a list of words in both French and English," he said sourly. "Truly remarkable, would you not say, Watson?" he turned to me and I stood in annoyance.

"Look here Holmes, this young lady is our guest. I must insist on your basic courtesy."

A faint sardonic smile shifted Holmes' face almost unpleasantly. "Ah, the bear has his bear baiter, I see. Very good, Watson. Yes, yes, quite right - I must heed your words."

He now turned to Miss Sully and bowed gracefully. "I do beg your pardon, Miss Sully. My impatience at times has the better of my manners. If you will forgive me, I beg you to continue."

I resumed my seat and Miss Sully resumed her tale, a little discomfited perhaps, but I noticed not offended as some of the more sensitive of her sex might have been at Holmes' rudeness.

Young Benniston had ceased the slow circling of his hat and after looking blankly at Holmes for a moment was now simply watching the young lady as she brought her reticule from the floor to her lap and opened the clasp. "Look," she said, holding out two folded slips of paper. "They are identical in paper, in ink, and most puzzling of all, in hand."

Holmes took up the notes and examined them swiftly before handing them to me. "What do you make of these, Watson?"

I was well used to Holmes testing me in this way. Many were the times I had heard his "you know my methods – apply them!" and just as many were the times I disappointed him with my inability to interpret my observations into a meaningful surmise. Or rather, perhaps I did not disappoint him. I had lately done a little reading in the rather interesting new field of what was beginning to be called psychoanalysis. The term 'egosim' had accrued a new meaning, and I rather suspected that some of the controversial Dr. Freud's insights might well prove to be accurate. I often caught myself wondering whether Holmes' encouragements to me were in fact nothing more than a wish – I will be frank - to humiliate me, and therefore feed his own considerable conceit.

Nevertheless, I took the two notes and played my dutiful part. "Common enough paper" I said, turning them over. "Could have been purchased anywhere. Rather unusual ink. I think perhaps continental in origin. And the hand is obviously that of man, not that of an invalid, and certainly not that of a woman." I handed them back to Holmes who took them with his customary bland look.

"Ah Watson, you have looked and not seen. I think you have missed every one of the most salient points." I shifted in my chair, not caring to hide my displeasure. "Common paper indeed," he went on, "but what is common paper in the West End of London is hardly common paper in a poor, French sanatorium. Similarly, unusual ink has its 'usual' locale. Miss Sully, you can confirm, can you not, that this hand is previously unknown to you?"

"Indeed I can, Mr. Holmes. In fact, I have brought one of my mother's letters to show you the difference." She once again opened her reticule and produced a letter, this time still in its envelope, and handed it up to Holmes.

"Excellent!" said Holmes. "Now we get on." There were a few moments of silence as Holmes produced from the inner pocket of his smoking jacket his brass telescopic magnifier and applied it to his eye as he scrutinised the letter written by the dead woman. Mr. Benniston shuffled his feet and looked from Miss Sully to me, with an enquiring glance. Miss Sully's eyes remained fixed upon Holmes; my own upon the parlour wall and the faintly discernable 'VR' made out in bullet holes now long since papered over. From below I could hear the newspaper boys beginning to call out the evening editions and the regular rattle of hansoms peppered with the occasional growl from a cab driver. A yellow, rather fetid evening had descended.

"Now, Miss Sully," began Holmes at last, refolding the letter and placing it back in the envelope. "Perhaps it is time you told us why you are really here, and why you have taken the trouble to invent this rather shabby tale, instead of telling us the truth."

My astonishment brought me again to my feet. "Holmes," I cried, "Have you taken leave of your senses as well as your civility? For heaven's sake, man, these young people have come to you for help."

But at this moment Mr. Benniston also stood and turned to Miss Sully. He reached for her hand and spoke in a low, fervid voice. "Catherine, you know our urgency. I cannot sit idly by while this man toys with us. I don't pretend to comprehend his game, but I do know we cannot wait upon it. Let us go immediately. We have failed here – we must now try my father."

Miss Sully took his hand and rose quickly, still clasping her reticule. "Thank you, Ralph. Of course, and this time we go together." They left the room with a brief nod to me but ignoring Holmes. He hadn't moved, save for his expression. As I examined it in my exasperation, I rather thought I could see something more complex than the derision I expected.

The moment we heard the street door slam, Holmes burst into activity, peeling off his smoking jacket and reaching for the greatcoat hanging rather unconventionally behind the door. "Quick Watson, not a moment to lose! Hat and coat, and we need that blessed Boots as well. They mustn't elude us."

A moment later we found ourselves in the damp and foggy street, still buttoning our coats and accompanied by Mrs. Hudson's young Boots. He had thought to protest but Holmes' production of a shilling purchased his silence and goodwill remarkably quickly. We saw the young couple entering a cab a few doors down and immediately secured another. The driver began with "'Ere, that young scamp can't ride inside along of you two gents! He'll have to hang on behind." Boots began to scramble out to comply – what boy would be content to sit inside a vehicle when he could cling on to the back? - but Holmes' purse again provided the détente, this time with the driver, who touched his whip to his hat in salute. Holmes asked him to follow the first cab discreetly and we set off.

"Now, Holmes, what is all this about? Where was the deception? They seemed to me to be an honest pair. What was in that letter?"

"Nothing was in the letter, save some banal comments about health and weather, and mild complaints about French food."

"What then? Why aren't we sitting by the fire with a pipe?"

Boots, who was somewhat cramped between Holmes' and my feet, was looking from one to the other of us, attempting meanwhile to tuck in the odd corner of undershirt peeping from beneath his buttoned jacket. Then he realised he was still holding the shilling, and he investigated his jacket for a pocket. Not finding one, he turned down the top of his stocking and pressed the shilling down towards his shoe.

Rather than reply to my rather irritated question, Holmes leant back and chuckled. I raised myself slightly to rap on the roof for the driver, for I had had enough, but before I could do so, Holmes grasped my wrist. "Watson, Watson," he said, shaking his head. "You are quite right; I have served you abominably this evening. Even the most abstemious of diets requires the occasional crumb. I will explain to you our reasons for pursuing young Miss Sully and young Mr. Benniston.

"Did you not think it odd that Miss Sully originally described the young man as her brother, yet gave him a different surname from her own? No? Well. And then there is the question of why she allowed her mother, a frail invalid, to travel alone overseas and yet later had no trouble making the trip herself for the rather trivial reason of asking a question?"

"But she explained herself," I replied. "She was not close to her mother. And I understood that her mother was not expected to die so soon. And as for the trivial question, why, that was almost a matter of life and death. As for the brother's name, she was merely extemporising and said the first thing that came into her head. Really, Holmes, I think this time you are reading rather too much into the situation. I believe your constant exposure to the most sordid elements of humanity might at last have tarnished your famous objcctivity."

Again Holmes chuckled. "Ah well," he said. "Perhaps that is so. We seem to have arrived, in any case, so let us have our wits about us." He then spoke a few urgent words to the Boots, who beamed, and with a quick salute licked his palm and drew it across his forelock before scrambling over our feet and jumping down, slamming the cab door behind him. Holmes leaned back, and rotating his hands, calmly inspected his nails, first one hand then the other, and said not a word. In frustration I crossed my arms, huffed, shifted my weight, and looked out the window at what little I could see of the London street through the dirty gloom.

Some five minutes later I was on the point of addressing Holmes about his unkept promise to explain to me what we were doing, when I heard above the background hum and scrape of street life, the quick steps of a running youngster. Sure enough, the Boots suddenly thrust his face through the window and whispered hoarsely "They're in and out, sir. They went in just as you said, and they came straight back out, and the lady's a-going to go on in the cab, sir, and the gentleman said he'd walk as how the night air would do him good, though how that's so I couldn't say, sir, as the fog's a regular monster tonight, sir, as my ma would say. Sir."

"Very good, young shaver," said Holmes appreciatively. He produced another shilling and held it up to the Boots' face. "And now this shilling says you can't trail the gentleman without him seeing you."

"Can't I though?" The young boy was delighted by the challenge, and with a parting glance at the coin in Holmes' hand, ducked away out of sight and up the street.

"Holmes, is it right to send a child into the streets at night? And what is he after anyway? Surely your conscience tells you of your duty to keep him safe?"

"Duty? My duty to Mrs. Hudson's Boots? He shall be two shillings ahead for the night's adventure and think himself the gainer in the bargain. There are times, my dear Watson, when your tendency to sentiment verges on the foolish."

I was now angry. Well used to Holmes' callousness as I was, the combination of his disregard for the child's safety and his wilful determination to keep me in ignorance left me ready to return home and leave him to his night's entertainment. I had just made up my mind to do so when the cab lurched into movement again. Of course – we were once more following the other cab, though this time it contained only Miss Sully.

This part of the journey was considerably longer, and with so many twists and turns I was quite soon disoriented. My ears told me that we were still travelling on London streets but as the fog by now obscured any details save the glow of the intermittent gas lamps, we might have been in Soho or in Clapham for all I knew.

I would not look at Holmes. The light inside the cab was dim but if the truth be known, it was fear of seeing scorn on his face that kept my gaze fixed on my own hands. And now I began to feel the familiar self-mocking, the scornful voice within asking me what held my tongue against this unkind treatment. I shook my head quickly and began to speak without thought. "So we follow Miss Sully. Do we know where she is headed? And what of Mr. Benniston – where is he leading our Boots? Do we expect a crisis?"

"No, Watson old friend. No crisis tonight." His voice was almost gentle as he turned to me. "Miss Sully we are merely escorting, as I perceive some little danger for her, and I wanted to be sure of her safe arrival back at her hotel but without her knowledge. She is, as you say, an honest young woman who applied to me for help."

"But Holmes, you said to me that you suspected her of deceit. That you questioned her story. You even said as much to the young lady herself!"

"Quite so. I regret to have caused you consternation. The fact is, Watson, that there are times my unfortunate character leads me to test my thoughts against your solid good sense, knowing full well that you dislike the confusion this brings. I am sure I owe you an apology, yet the value of such must be considerably diminished when one considers the surfeit over these many years."

I shifted uncomfortably. There it was again. The man needed me, I understood that. After all, his was an unusual gift and it seemed my lot to help him as I could. I sighed. "And Mr. Benniston?"

"Ah, young Mr. Benniston indeed. I fear the twists of this one will both sadden and surprise the young people. A complex and yet very simple set of circumstances."

"You are talking in riddles, Holmes." But he turned to the darkened window in silence.

When we found ourselves back at Baker Street some half hour later, I was relieved to see the young Boots open the door to us. He looked none the worse for his escapade and brightened further as Holmes slipped the second shilling, and I thought, a note, into his hand. They exchanged a whispered word or two and it occurred to me that this was probably not the first time Holmes had engaged his services. Mrs. Hudson and I were certainly familiar with the occasionally visits from Holmes' urchin Irregulars, but I felt certain she was not aware of his recruiting of her own household staff. For a moment I considered my responsibility in the matter, then dismissed the thought and followed Holmes up the stairs to the parlour.

The fire had been recently stirred, the lamps were lit and a cold collation was set out on the tea table. Holmes and I set to, and a little later we settled by the fire, Holmes with his old briar and me with the small Indian cigarettes I had recently taken to smoking. I cleared my throat to ask, with all the firmness I could rally, what the meaning of the night's adventure had indeed been, when Holmes broke in.

"I am expecting a visitor, Watson. Any time now, I should say."

"Indeed? I shall withdraw."

"By no means, old chap. I am convinced you would like to be in at the denouement, shall we say, of our little tale."

"Good heavens - you mean it is Miss Sully you expect?"

"No indeed, not Miss Catherine Sully. And no, before you ask, not Mr. Ralph Benniston. I think we shall receive … but wait, if I am not mistaken, here he is."

At that, we heard the street door and two sets of steps mounting the stairs. A sharp rap on the parlour door and Boots entered, followed by a stout, bewhiskered gentleman with a distinctly commercial air and a slip of paper in his hand. “Mr. Arthur Benniston, sir, to see you if you please, sir,” said Boots, and he ducked away.

Holmes rose with outstretched hand. “Ah, very good of you to call, Mr. Benniston, on such a raw night and at such an hour.”

“What the devil – just who the devil are you, sir?” The gentleman did not take Holmes’ hand. His face was flushed, and I observed as he stood a slight swaying. His chin was thrust up belligerently and his pale side whiskers stuck out like rough stooks. “Well? You say my son is mixed up in something.” He waved the note. “What is it and where is your proof?”

“I must beg your pardon, Mr. Benniston. I regret that a slight untruth was necessary to ensure your interest. It is not your son who has erred but yourself.” At this the man’s rubicund countenance reddened further and he raised his hands in what looked for a moment like a pugilist’s reflex. I rose swiftly and stood next to Holmes. “I must warn you,” I began, but Holmes smiled benignantly at me. “Thank you, Watson, but I believe I am no danger from this man.” He turned to Mr. Benniston. “Sir, I will come to the point. You wrote a letter anonymously to Miss Catherine Sully implying that she was your illegitimate daughter. This was not true. Would you care to explain to my friend Dr. Watson here why you would do such a thing?”

The ruddy faced gentleman scowled for a moment, then subsided, and indeed, guided by Holmes, he dropped into a chair. He drew a deep and ragged sigh.

"He's my only boy. Any father would do the same. Well now, it's like this. Ralph is to take over the mill when he is of age and it's always been my wish that he marry well." He paused, and with his drooping hands loosely clenched, he looked up at us. "I know what I am, Mr. Holmes. You don't shake those roots, try as you might, and I wanted better for Ralph. My wife," he paused, and shook his head like a dog with a grass seed in its ear. "My wife is a better soul, sir, and I am not ashamed somehow to say that she saw fit to leave me when young Ralph left for Cambridge. And then when I saw the way the wind blew with Ralph and young Miss Catherine, why I had my idea. It didn't feel right at first and that's God's truth. But it was like a bad angel, whispering at me. So I did it. I didn't know that poor woman, the one who died. But I knew who she was all right, because I knew young Miss Catherine.

"Miss Catherine came and worked for me, you see. I wouldn't hold with this at first, of course, a young lady working in a mill! Why, that's no place. But with my wife on at me in one ear about rights for women and look at the antipodes where women have the vote now! And Ralph in the other ear about what a capable person was Catherine, and just the thing the secretaries' room needed, well in the end I took her on. And to be fair to the lass, I had no cause to regret my decision when it came to her work. But soon enough I heard the whispers around the place; why were the dirty jobs given to the women? Why were they paid less than the men? And on and on. I could see that Catherine was a minx and she would turn my mill topsy turvey if I didn't look about me. This was not the wife for my son. I wanted my mill to be in a fit state for him to take over, and I wanted him to be in a fit state to *take* it over. So whichever way I examined the case, young Miss Catherine had to go.

"Yet, if I relieved her of her duties, I knew that would only serve to seal it between them. The way I began to see it was that if the two of them believed there were half brother and sister, why, there's an end to it. Done. And if they confronted me with it, I could deny it all I liked but the idea would be there, gnawing at them. Even if young Miss Catherine decided to keep mum about the letter, I knew she wouldn't go ahead and marry young Ralph with that thought in her head. So I wrote the letter." He lifted his chin and took a deep breath in. "I wrote the letter and I fear I may lose my son over it." He blinked quickly and employed the back of his hand to clear his eyes. "Though how you know it was me I'll be blessed if I can say."

Holmes took a thoughtful pace across the face of the fire and turned towards Mr. Benniston.

"There is one thing you might clear up for me. You wrote to Mrs. Sully in France, I believe?"

At this, Mr. Benniston started and looked at Holmes with fear. "What makes you say that?"

"Why, there was a slip of French translations in her things."

"I don't know anything about that! Nothing at all. Why would I write to *her*? The plan was to write to Catherine, that's all. An anonymous letter to Miss Catherine"

"And how interesting that Mrs. Sully died so unexpectedly, before her daughter could ask her about that letter."

"But she was ill. She had consumption."

"Not quite so ill, I believe. It is almost as though something sped her along."

Benniston felt quickly for the arms of the chair and pushed himself upright. The pugilist had returned in an instant. "What are you saying?" he thrust his flushed face into Holmes'. "What do you mean, you blackguard?"

Holmes held his ground calmly. "Perhaps if I apply to the nuns at a certain French sanatorium I will find that a special parcel of English food arrived for Mrs. Sully shortly before her death. A parcel from an anonymous benefactor. A parcel of foods she found herself missing during her continental convalescence."

The red faced Bennsiton emitted what could only be called a growl, and stumbling against the chair, he flung himself through the door and downstairs.

After the thump of the street door, silence settled in the parlour. My thoughts ran through what I had just heard. "But Holmes," I said, "how in Heaven's name did you know he had sent something to Mrs. Sully. And do I take you to mean that he *poisoned* Catherine's mother?"

"Sadly, that is precisely what I believe he did. The list of words translated from English to French and written by the same hand that wrote the singularly malicious letter included words solely related to the serving of food." I recalled the slip of paper and nodded.

"I rather fancy he wrote a note to the nuns accompanying the gift of food. As we have seen, he is a self-made man without the benefit of a gentleman's education, so for him to write a note in French was no small feat. He had recourse to a French English dictionary, and the slip of paper was an *aide memoire* that was then accidentally included in the parcel Mrs. Sully received. I fear that something in the parcel, innocently prepared for her by the nuns, hastened her end."

"And Mrs. Sully retained the slip of paper. Perhaps she meant to ask the nuns about it," I mused.

"Perhaps she did. At any rate, it puzzled her enough to keep. But without seeing Catherine's letter, it would not alarm her."

"But Holmes, why did you send the two of them away from here so harshly? Your behaviour was abominable."

"I hazarded your displeasure because I wanted them to lose no time in seeking out the elder Mr. Benniston and I saw my way clear to do so swiftly. We needed to follow them unobserved to be certain, and because I believed there was a chance of our whiskered friend finding a way to do more harm tonight."

"Miss Catherine?"

"Indeed. Once I had inferred the source and reason for the letter, I saw his motive and it boded ill for both the consumptive and her daughter. You observed how brief the young couple's visit was to him? He turned them out with somewhat vulgar haste even by my abominable standards." At this, Holmes cast me a sidelong, almost sheepish look.

"But Miss Catherine will be safe now?"

"Oh yes. The horse has bolted from this particular stable. Our rather unpleasant bully knows we have his measure, and after all, his plan has now failed." Holmes stood and reached for the Persian slipper to refill his pipe. "Tomorrow by the first post Miss Catherine will receive an anonymous letter withdrawing the earlier claim and thus clearing the way for the two to marry, or whatever it is that young people do."

"I suppose this letter will be in a different hand," I ventured. "On different paper?"

Holmes chuckled. "Indeed. Pass me that inkwell, my dear chap, and ring for Mrs. Hudson if you would be so good. I believe she is still up and I rather fancy some cognac after all."

# The Case of the Unexpected Dog

## The Case of the Unexpected Dog

A copy of The Lancet lay on the divan beside me. I had dropped it with a sigh and was now gazing abstractedly at the miniature of our queen on the sideboard.

My old injury had returned to haunt me in recent weeks, and its nagging ache prohibited my usual activities. A yellowish, afternoon gloom seeped through the half-open curtains. Not for the first time I considered whether I might be better employed establishing myself back in civilian medical practice than lounging uncomfortably in the drawing room at Baker Street. When I had tentatively hinted at this to Holmes a week or so prior, he had dismissed me with a "By all means, you must do whatever you choose," before returning to the abstruse details of the case he had then been engaged upon.

But what *did* I choose? The excitement of being drawn into Holmes' cases, punctuated though they were by periods of stultifying inactivity, had spoiled me for a regular and predictable occupation. The idea of seeing a succession of dull patients with their pedestrian complaints paralysed me with boredom. And of course, I would have to leave Baker Street to set up rooms somewhere. I had no confidence that I could establish a regular list of patients, being so long out of civilian practice and never a particularly sociable man. Perhaps I could assist a doctor whose practice had grown too large to manage single-handed. Perhaps I could find a hamlet somewhere where the local doctor was retiring. Yet the prospect of a quiet village life filled me with dismay. I sighed again.

Taken all around, I had to confess that I was drifting without purpose. Since my return from military service, I no longer felt my worth as I had when serving my sovereign and country. I had gradually allowed myself to depend upon Holmes for those sharp periods of excitement that gave my existence its savour and indeed a semblance of meaning. But perhaps most germane was the fact that I had been suffering from some little financial constraint for the past months. Like many another Britisher, I had been unfortunate in an insurance investment the previous year and had come within a hair's breadth of losing my service pension entirely. As it was, I had been lucky to escape with an adequate, though modest, allowance. Plainly, it was time for me to make some sort of a change.

I continued my vacillating musing until I was interrupted by a thunderous knock at the street door. I heard the Boots' hurried steps from the back of the house followed by raised voices. Somewhat surprised, I roused myself from the divan to go down to assist. I heard Mrs. Hudson's voice expostulate, then the sound of the stairs taken two at a time, and the drawing room door burst open.

"No, you can't, sir!" cried Mrs. Hudson, as a roughly dressed, bearded man followed a very large and shaggy dog into the room.

"Can't I though?" said the man. "I have my orders, same as you, missus. The gentleman told me to bring Barghest right in here and leave him in charge of the other gentleman." At this he nodded in my direction. "Afternoon sir. Here is Barghest as promised." With that the man untied a piece of cord from around the dog's neck, turned and descended the stairs two at a time. The front door slammed.

Mrs. Hudson and I looked in astonishment at one another, and then at the dog, which shook itself vigorously and lay down on the hearth. I became aware of an aroma redolent of things long dead, animal and vegetable.

"Did you…" began Mrs. Hudson.

"I did not!"

"It'll be Mr. Holmes, then, sir".

"Yes, I rather think that is what it will be."

We turned to look again at the dog. It was large, certainly, and filthy, but its most striking feature was its attitude of ease. It had paid not the slightest attention to its escort as the man left and was now bestowing an equal disregard on Mrs. Hudson and me. It laid its rough head on its paws and appeared to doze.

"Well, I suppose we must just wait until Holmes returns," I said uncertainly. "No doubt there is an excellent reason behind this. The dog is crucial in some current investigation, or..."

Mrs Hudson sniffed ostentatiously. “You think so, Dr. Watson? You think Mr. Holmes only acts with ‘excellent’ reason? Well, begging your pardon, sir, but I suggest you open those eyes of yours, just as you must open that window.”

Mrs. Hudson abruptly turned and quitted the room, closing the door firmly behind her.

She was quite right: the window must be opened immediately.

I had not seen Holmes for some days and had no idea where he might be nor upon what mission he was currently engaged. There was no way to reach him: he was not a club man, nor did he maintain a circle of friends with whom he could be staying. He was most ccrtainly on a case, which meant he might not reappear at Baker Street for days to come. I looked at the dog. I knew that it could not remain here without Mrs. Hudson taking some sort of dire action, yet I could not send it away without risking Holmes’ displeasure.

I had no alternative but to ignore my lingering pain and take the dog for a walk.

Barghest was an amiable if unruly walking companion. I had fastened some curtain cord that Mrs. Hudson found for me into a makeshift yoke, and we made our way along the embankment, me limping and Barghest stopping and starting, sniffing, looping back and entangling the cord.

When we finally returned, there had still been no sign of Holmes, so with Mrs. Hudson's permission I commissioned Boots to take the dog down into the area with some buckets of water and soap. It was a rowdy bath: I could hear the shouts of the boy and the splashing of water from upstairs where I had resumed my place in the drawing room. Eventually there was a knock at the door and a wet and dishevelled Boots led in a much cleaner but still disreputable-looking dog.

"He's clean now sir," said Boots with pride. "See? There's even white on his paws. He's a very clever dog, sir," he added confidentially. "Will Mr. Holmes be a keeping of him?"

"I don't know," I replied. "I don't quite know what he is *for*."

"Well, he is very clever all the same, sir, and I beg you to tell Mr. Holmes so." The boy cast a lively glance at the dog, which acknowledged him not at all, and quitted the room whistling under his breath, explicitly against Mrs. Hudson's firm household rule. To my astonishment, the dog lurched up onto the divan, gave a luxurious yawn and settled down for a doze.

"Well, Barghest old fellow," I said as I filled and lit my pipe, "I believe you know something that I do not. Perhaps I will take the basket chair this time, if it is all the same to you."

The unconventional Barghest accompanied me again the following morning, this time for a stroll in Regent's Park. As dogs went, his manners were mild, and in spite of Boots' protestations, I felt that his purported cleverness was perhaps also rather mild. He expressed only a slight interest in squirrels, birds, lapdogs and horses, which made him an easy though unstimulating companion. I found my aches were improving; it was a couple of hours before we returned to Baker Street.

There was still no word from Holmes, and although he did not make an appearance all throughout that day, I did at least receive confirmation that he was actively working on a case. I always found myself becoming uneasy after an absence on his part of more than a day or so, thus it was with something of relief that I received a telegram that read simply "Blue canvas bag and stick tropical diseases 1pm stop. Not dog stop".

I collected the bag and the stick from Holmes' room, and leaving Barghest once again sleeping on the divan, I made my way to the West End to deliver my commission and seek an answer to the question of the dog. My hopes of seeing Holmes himself were dashed, however: I was met at the bottom of the steps to the University of London's School of Tropical Diseases by a familiar member of Holmes' Baker Street Irregulars.

"Dobson," I said. "Is Mr. Holmes here?"

The boy looked conspiratorially up and down the street and touched the side of his nose. "No sir, don't know the gentleman if you please sir. Thank you, sir." And with that, he took the bag and the stick and was gone, racing off in the direction whence I had just arrived.

I stood irresolute for a moment, recognising a familiar helplessness swell in my breast. Holmes! I determined not to surrender to my frustrations, however. Instead I would occupy my own time for a little while. I looked about me: Bloomsbury. The Museum? A stroll in The Square perhaps? Or luncheon? Indeed, I had had nothing since breakfast and my long walk with Barghest had piqued my appetite. The Hotel Russell was nearby. I decided that some beef and Yorkshire pudding and a half bottle of good claret would be an excellent distraction for the afternoon.

It was almost three o'clock when I arrived back at Baker Street. A sullen Boots let me in, and I made my own way up through what my fancy told me was a rather oppressively silent house to the drawing room.

The dog was gone. I rang for Mrs. Hudson, who started to speak before she was in the room. "You must see as I had no choice, sir, as such a smelly beast and no house manners which fact I came close to giving notice to you gents." She was clearly upset and repeatedly drew a handkerchief through her looped finger and thumb. "I'm sorry Dr. Watson, sir. It's not you as I object to, as you well know, sir. You have always spoke up for me, but it's the explosions and the smells and now this as is worse than an open sewer, so it had to go, sir."

"Mrs. Hudson, where is the dog?"

“On its way to Hampstead, sir, as soon as the carrier arrives. My sister has a market garden and she will take the creature. It’s tied up in the area, just now, and blessed if Cook hasn’t given it one of my soup bones. Boots is beside his young self and we are all at sixes and sevens.”

“Mrs Hudson, you know I would do anything in my power to make your life comfortable and I am sorry the dog has been a nuisance, but Holmes needs it for something of significance and we really must keep it. I will undertake some responsibility, and if you can spare Boots every now and again, I’m sure between us we can keep the thing out of mischief until we know what purpose Holmes has. Here is a sovereign for the carrier, and I will come down with you now and bring the creature upstairs.”

Eventually Mrs. Hudson allowed herself to be persuaded. I brought Barghest back up to the drawing room and he quietly took his place on the divan with a grunt of comfort. I sat by him and patted his shaggy head. “Well, old fellow,” I said, “whatever it is, it must be important. If only you could speak, eh?”

He stretched out all four ungainly legs with a quivering sigh and closed his eyes. I picked up my Lancet and settled myself to read.

Some hours later I was startled by the slamming of the street door, and I heard what sounded like Holmes’ tread ascending the stairs. I stood and gathered my irritations and grievances together to accost him the moment he entered. I heard his steps pass the drawing room door and continue to his own room, and then the brisk snick of the door closing. "Oh, I don't believe so," I thought. "You owe me an explanation, sir." Barghest roused himself and followed me as I went through to the hall and rapped on Holmes' door.

"Holmes!" I said. "You must come out and explain yourself."

There was a pause and the sound of movement, then Holmes' voice calling out, "Ah, Watson. Just the fellow. I shall join you in a moment."

"No need, old boy," I said, "I can join you," and I opened his door.

He was sitting on his bed wearing a rough calico jacket, torn at the arms and deeply stained. His bleeding hands rested in his lap, his muddied trousers were tied at the waist with rope and his boots were heavy and wet. He looked up at me through a swollen face almost unrecognisable in its yellow and indigo bruising, puffy eyes lined with dried blood and an immoderately split lip.

"Good God, Holmes!" I exclaimed. "Whatever have you been doing?"

He twisted his face into a painful half grin. "Winning, Watson. Winning."

I stood stunned and without speech. At that moment I felt Barghest push up to my side.

"Ah," said Holmes. "And here is your dog." I thought I detected a twinkle in his half-closed eye. "Tell me Watson, did you notice anything unusual about the man who brought him here?"

"Why no, just a navvy, rather ill mannered - " I broke off. There was silence for a moment. "Good Heavens!" I exclaimed. "It was you, Holmes! How could I be such a fool?" Holmes smiled to himself and made no answer.

I dressed Holmes' injuries to the best of my abilities. It took considerable professional finesse on my part to induce him to remove his jacket and shirt so that I might examine him. He was badly bruised and in spite of his innate stoicism I could see he was in some pain, wincing and giving little hisses of breath as I gently felt his ribs – not, I believed, broken – and back. Finally, in a loose shirt and smoking jacket, he settled gingerly into the basket chair and lit his briar. The bandages on his hands gave him some little difficulty and I ruefully mused that they would surely be removed by morning.

It was evident that Holmes had been quite savagely beaten. Since he could be relied upon to give a good account of himself in a physical contest, I concluded that he had been set upon by a gang, in a no doubt organised assault, presumably in retaliation against some successful investigations he was pursuing. But before I could commence my barrage of questions, Holmes spoke.

"Now Watson, I believe you have been contemplating that removal, and a return to medical practice."

"Well, I'll be dashed!" I exclaimed. I had been at pains to keep my uncomfortable thoughts to myself since Holmes' rebuff. "Look here, you must know that I have no wish to do so. The fact is that I am experiencing a little …"

"Yes, yes, times are difficult at present." Holmes winced as he stretched his legs out in front of him, and I inwardly regretted that I had failed to persuade him to submit to a complete examination. "As it happens, I believe I might be able to suggest a very suitable situation for you. What would you say to being paid a week's salary for a few hours' medical work, every week or so?"

"I would say, some law is being broken somewhere, and I have no wish to jeopardise my reputation, such as it is, by becoming entangled in it."

Holmes chuckled, and instantly winced. I had warned him that his ribs would become more painful over the next few days, before the bruising began to settle, and I wondered how he would accommodate this pain in his often-vigorous life.

"My dear Watson, you are indeed an example of that stalwart foundation upon which our great empire rests. However, what would you say if I told you that your involvement, for let us say, no more than three weeks, would considerably assist me in my present case, the outcome of which could have quite significant implications." At this he glanced at Her Majesty's portrait on the sideboard, and I understood him to mean that these were grave matters of state in which I could play my patriotic part.

In short, I allowed him to persuade me.

Holmes, it seemed, had spent many weeks infiltrating a rather secretive boxing establishment. He was convinced it was operated by an enigmatic character who had been implicated in a series of elaborate frauds. These frauds involved a senior MP, who in turn had been leading some high-level negotiations with the government of a nation with whom we had at best an uneasy alliance. The situation was delicate in the extreme, and Holmes had gradually been penetrating the outer circles of protection, making his way closer to the heart of the operation.

"Who is this character?" I asked. "Have I heard of him?"

"I doubt that your somewhat retired life would have brought you into contact with her." My intake of breath was sharp. "However, you might well have heard of one or two of her aliases. Kitty Baxter, also known as Mary Amelia Johnson, and I believe a year or so ago, presenting around town as Lord Felix Anderson."

"Lord Anderson! Why, that's the fellow who gave his patronage to that cursed insurance scheme. I was mercilessly duped there, Holmes, and I have suffered for my foolhardiness, but far worse than my circumstances are those of some of his victims. I have heard of families made all but destitute, while those swindlers made away with their savings." I paused for a moment as Holmes' words penetrated my thoughts. "But, look here, you're saying that Lord Anderson is nothing but a crook, *and* that he is a woman!"

"Indeed, I am certain that Lord Anderson is the invention of Kitty Baxter, as also, I suspect, was the Capital Insurance and Loan. I believe I am getting close, but my approach has been a rather circuitous one. I also have adopted an alias, in my case taking a few steps down the social ladder rather than up. Allow me to introduce myself: Jacob Rouse, bare knuckle up-and-coming, lately arrived from Nova Scotia."

"And that of course explains your condition. But Holmes, have a care! As your friend, and perhaps I can also say as your doctor, I must caution you that this approach carries considerable risks. Why, look at the state you are in! And you said you had been winning. I dread to consider what you will look like if you commence losing."

Again, Holmes chuckled and winced. "Let me explain your duties," he said, ignoring my plaint. "You will be present at ten or a dozen matches in an evening and might be called upon to minster to the more badly damaged of the contestants. It is a matter of honour in this particular circle that medical attention is refused, so it is not uncommon for men injured quite seriously to make their way home as best they might, and seek what comfort there is to be found there. There has emerged a desire, however, among those organising these little gatherings, to have a doctor present. It seems that a death will always jeopardise these enterprises and it is thought that medical attention instantly available might forestall such an unfortunate circumstance. I have offered your services, and this has greatly assisted my efforts to ingratiate myself."

"By name Holmes? You have named me?"

"Good heavens, no. I don't believe a single gentleman, or indeed lady, who is involved in these contests goes by their real name. You are to be the Barghest doctor."

"The dog!"

"The dog. The dog will accompany you as a mascot, if you will. Barghest is well-known at the premises, though he belongs to no one. In fact it was I who named him, after the mythological beast of Yorkshire of which you might have heard, though from what I have observed of his character, I believe a kitten might have been closer to the mark."

I laughed. "Indeed, he is gentle creature," I said, scratching the sleepy dog's head. "And I am reminded that I bear a message for you, concerning him: Barghest is, according to Boots, a very clever dog."

At this we both laughed, and looking at the comfortable, drowsy beast stretched along the divan, I reflected that perhaps he was clever after all. Against chance, he had found himself a most suitable situation: perhaps I was about to do the same.

I had of course attended one or two boxing matches in the past, and during my military service had frequently witnessed young soldiers organising a few rounds in their leisure hours. But these tame examples of Queensbury Rules had not prepared me for the vicious brawling that was an unofficial bareknuckle match. I thanked heaven that Holmes was not yet fit to fight again, for I don't believe I could have tolerated watching him take part in such brutal encounters.

The fights took place in an expansive hall behind a temperance society office in Shepherds Bush. Entry was controlled by a pair of lump-eared, shirtless ruffians at a side door, and payment was by production of a penny, or in my case, of Barghest. Holmes accompanied me in his costume as Jacob, somewhat displaying his bandages, and we made our way to a corner under the stairs, quite near the makeshift ring. Barghest settled in the sawdust at my feet and dozed, oblivious to the cacophony of shouts, cries, huzzahs and curses that was unrelenting from the moment we arrived until we were able to make our way out some three hours later.

I witnessed a round dozen of the dreadful encounters. In nine of these, the match was eventually won when a contestant knocked his opponent to the ground unconscious. The injured man was quickly carried off and brought to me, where his friends, or I regret to say, on some occasions his wife, would then insist the unconscious fellow was perfectly well, calling up some extra pairs of hands to carry him home. Two matches were decided by the pugilists themselves, who after interminable rounds, agreed that the result was a draw. The final match, I say without exaggeration, left me ashamed to be an Englishman. The winner, for so he was, had aimed a deliberate and savage blow up under his opponent's solar plexus and then kicked the man's legs from under him. I rose from my seat in consternation when the poor fellow hit the floorboards heavily. He raised himself up on his elbows but was unable to crawl to scratch, and the place erupted in cheering and laughter as the careless crowd settled their wagers.

The downed man was brought to me semi-conscious. I tended his as best I could but I feared his internal injuries were serious. "Holmes," I said. "This man needs a hospital."

Holmes hissed at me. "Jacob!" he said. "Jacob is my name! And no, I doubt there is any chance of that. There is no hospital for the likes of these men." Then he lifted his head and speaking apparently for the benefit of those nearby, said, "Do your best, doctor. The man is poorly, that's sure, for that were a masterful hit."

Eventually the man, a little recovered but not yet able to stand unaided, was helped out through a separate door by one of the ill-favoured gentlemen who had allowed us entry. The door was closed.

It was evident that Holmes, in his character as Jacob, was well known by those in attendance; ill-bred working men and well-dressed gentry alike. They would stop by our alcove and greet him, with a joke and a laugh. "Not fighting tonight then, Jacob? That there Marcus was one too many for you then? Still, you are coming along quite tidy for such a lean one." After one such exchange, Holmes leaned in towards me and whispered tersely, "That is the one. His name is Lewis. He controls who gets in to see Baxter. If I can just convince him –" he broke off as a ruddy-faced, gentlemanly man swayed to a stop in the company of a couple of young dandies.

"Jacob, by my life," said the gentleman hoarsely. "Broken, eh? Next time then."

"And that," said Holmes quietly as the man, followed by his acolytes, slowly made his way into the throng, "is our rather slippery MP. I mean to run him to ground."

From time to time Holmes would leave me to make his way into the disorderly crowd. I watched him engage in what appeared to be uncharacteristically hilarious banter with some of the men and on occasion this intercourse would shift into hasty and secretive exchanges. It was clear that he progressed. I on the other hand, was somewhat miserable, consoling myself with the thought that I was materially assisting this important case.

Barghest remained relaxed throughout, and I was amused to see how many of these coarsened and rough individuals were fond of the dog. They would pass our alcove and stoop to give him a pat or a kind word. By association, they were well-disposed toward me as well. "All right, there, doctor?" they would say genially, or offer me a swig from the thick bottles they kept safe in their inner pockets.

I was relieved when Holmes gave me the signal that we might depart, though the fights had not yet finished. I understood that only the less important contests were still to run, and clearly those combatants did not require medical attendance. As we made our way back to the door at the side, one of the men on duty there thrust a handful of grubby notes at me. I took them self-consciously and folded and secreted them.

Back at Baker Street, Barghest and I collapsed onto the divan and Holmes handed me a large whisky.

"Well, Watson, how did you enjoy your evening's divertissement?"

"Holmes," I groaned. "Amuse yourself at my expense as you like, but tell me, must I return to that hellhole?"

"You must, old fellow, but I am in hopes that one more visit will do it. Wednesday next, you, the dog and I will again take our places, and I rather think I will be admitted to the sanctum sanctorum, in which case I shall soon bring this matter to a close. Incidentally, old man, I rely on you to make sure I do not yet look fit to fight."

At this I laughed, for in truth he was not likely to be in any state for fighting for a week at least, however I fancied that his pride was in conflict with his reason. He had told me himself that it was a matter of honour for the pugilists to refuse medical treatment, yet knowing him as I did, I felt he did not wish to exclude himself from the contest.

Holmes continued absent for the next few days and the while I found myself becoming accustomed to Barghest's company. The walks were improving my condition daily. It was not just the old wound: I felt my spirits lighten as we set out along the embankment or through St James Park. Barghest was an unprepossessing creature, and his appearance often caused young ladies to gasp or draw their skirts away, and I would boldly call out "It's all right, miss, he is quite safe." Young men would turn to take a second, amused look and small boys would follow in awe and ask me, "Does he rat, sir?"

Even Mrs. Hudson was tolerating his presence in our rooms. She certainly grumbled, but there were no more threats to send him to Hampstead, and I had reason to believe that on more than one occasion she had offered him dainties that Holmes and I had not seen at our table.

As Wednesday approached, I began to feel increasingly uneasy. I believed there would be danger, and this I was accustomed to, but I felt hampered by my ignorance of the situation and of the protagonists. Yet it was ever thus: Holmes had not confided his intentions to me. Whether he expected to seize evidence or restrain a criminal, I remained in the dark. I resolved to carry my service revolver with me.

Great was my relief when on the Tuesday evening, as I sat peacefully after dinner in the drawing room, a dreaming Barghest at my feet, I heard a sharp rap on the street door followed a few moments later by the Boots, making way for a bustling Lestrade.

"Dr. Watson, pleasure to see you, sir. And dog, I see."

Barghest had dreamily raised his head, opened an eye at Lestrade, and gone back to sleep. I shook Lestrade by the hand and told him he was most welcome, inviting him to sit. I apologised for Holmes' absence, but to my surprise he told me that it was me he wanted to see. He perched at the front of the basket chair, leaning forward and keeping his hat firmly in both hands. "I suppose you know all about it, Doctor?"

"Well, perhaps a little. Do you mean this Baxter woman?"

He nodded sagely. "Baxter, Johnson, Anderson and a few others besides, men and woman both, makes no odds. Quite an operation. But we mean to bust it, all right. I hear you are right in the thick of it yourself?" I explained my role to Lestrade, and he laughed immoderately. "That's pretty work for a gentleman such as yourself," he said. "Shame to waste your doctoring on ruffians and riff-raff like those. They deserve all that comes their way, you may be sure, sir."

"Look here," I said. "I am not so sure. I fancy some of these men are desperate to make a pound or two, and they end up being dragged home with a split liver and a broken nose, with no chance of hospital, and I dare say no chance of work for a good while, either. I must say I found the experience disquieting."

Lestrade sighed, still amused. "Well, well," he said. "That's as may be. Perhaps it will comfort you to know, then, Dr. Watson, that I will have half a dozen good men in at the fight tomorrow night, disguised of course, and ready to seize this Baxter and her henchmen. Your Mr. Holmes has been feeding us quite a good bit of information these last weeks and I do believe we are ready to act."

I was greatly relieved to hear Lestrade's words, but I resolved to carry my service revolver, nevertheless.

Holmes, Barghest and I were once again ensconced in the alcove, while the assorted and rowdy crowd filled the air with tobacco smoke, the smell of sweat, the sound of jeers and cheers and the thumps and groans of the fights themselves. I felt queasy with anticipation. Once again my duties were light, if you can call it light for a medical man to watch helplessly as fit and healthy men delivered themselves to the alter of crude might, and moments later left the ring with, often as not, broken bones that no one would be setting.

Holmes disappeared into the crowd as before, and I soon saw that he was deep in conversation with the man he had identified as Lewis. Holmes appeared to laugh wildly at some comment, then I watched as Lewis led him through the crush to the second door.

Lewis knocked and I saw them admitted by a particularly surly and ill-bred looking ruffian.

I settled back uncomfortably to wait and cast an eye on the fight that was commencing. Just as a very young-looking lad was thrown down to an eruption of cheers from the crowd, I saw a sudden movement from several quarters. There was jostling and angry shouts as several hefty fellows, no doubt Lestrade's men, pushed their way swiftly to the door that had admitted Holmes.

I leapt up and immediately made my way in the same direction. I feared for Holmes' safety, and I thrust my hand into my pocket as I pushed forward, so that I might feel the reassurance of my revolver. I reached the door before Lestrade's men and shoved it open, shouldering my way inside the room. I saw the tableau in an instant: A burly thug held Holmes from behind with his elbows locked in a tight grip, while another leaned in towards him holding a vicious knife inches from Holmes' throat and a third man held aloft an ugly club. To the side stood a tall, cloaked figure, leaning back against a table and smiling.

For one surreal instant, all was frozen, then the smile dropped from the face of the leaning figure, the thugs faced me in blank amazement; Lestrade's men, who had now thrust their way into the room, stopped dead.

"Release him," I said, and raised my weapon.

At that moment, an explosion of movement at my side burst upward to the man holding the knife, and as Barghest launched himself at the ruffian's throat, the thug holding the upraised club brought it down with full force. Barghest dropped to the ground, stone dead.

I was returning to Baker Street one mild afternoon some three months later. I had been walking, as was now my fixed habit, in Regent's Park, my old injury quiet and my heart becoming gradually more restored. I had been sorely grieved by the death of the dog, not least because Barghest had shown us in his last moments the measure of his quiet valour. It was not only courage, for I had come to Boots' way of thinking. I was now of the belief that Barghest had understood a great deal of what had transpired, and even that he understood the consequences of his terrible final spring. His placid good nature did indeed disguise a clever dog.

The same could not in truth be said of the noisy terrier pup that greeted me as Boots opened the street door.

"No quieter, I see. Not learning her lessons?"

"Well sir, she's doing the best she can, I suppose," he said, as he scooped the pup up. "I told Mrs. H, sir, these foxies don't amount to much indoors. She wants a rat or a rabbit hole, she does, but Mrs. H won't let me take her to the heath. Afraid she'll get dirty like as not." He raised his small chin in disgust, but as I took the stairs, I saw him put his cheek to the happily wriggling pup and close his eyes with a smile.

Holmes was home, and at his ease on the divan, perusing the Times. "Ah, Watson," he said as I shook off my coat. I see you have taken your usual route. How is the park?"

"Well, you know," I replied as I settled into the basket chair, "it is a little colourless without my erstwhile companion, but very pleasant nonetheless, and most refreshing after a morning indoors with McPherson's patients. They tend to the more irritable complaints of age, I am afraid. I am not surprised he felt the need of a holiday, but I can certainly manage these few days. And in fact, I think he will probably need some more regular help once he returns – his list is certainly growing. If he offers it to me, I shall certainly take it."

"Excellent, Watson, excellent. You have indeed regained something of your former vigour and ease."

"I have. You know, I credit this change to the dog, Holmes. His gentle company distracted me from my preoccupations, and I am the better for it."

"However, I believe the colony of New South Wales will be the worse for it. Our friend Miss Baxter is headed thither, according to the paper."

I had seen the article. It was remarkably brief for such a complex situation with no mention being made, I noted, of the involvement of a peer of the realm in the frauds and semi-legal enterprises of Kitty Baxter's empire.

"And how goes your committee?" he asked me.

"Fair. I have convinced one or two of my former colleagues to join us, and as one of them is resident surgeon at St Barts, I have a measure of confidence that our little enterprise will get on. The charitable side is being managed by some ladies known to him, and we speak to the Hospital Board of Governors tomorrow."

"Well done, old boy. So, the injured bare-knuckle ruffians will at last have somewhere to go to be patched up until the next week"

"Laugh if you like, Holmes, but think of those working men injured at the wharves or in the factories. This little plan will be a welcome one for their families, I am certain." I reached for my pipe and began to fill it. "At all events, Holmes, I have been considering – "

"I shouldn't do it if I were you. They are undignified for a gentleman of your years, and what if you should fall?"

"Good heavens, Holmes. I didn't say a word to you. How can you know what I had in mind?"

Holmes laughed, and shook out the pages of the paper, holding a quarter section towards me. "I see the three advertisements that have been circled in green ink – your green ink, Watson – are all propounding the virtues of the new safety bicycles. Ergo, my comment: I wouldn't do it if I were you."

I laughed. Elementary indeed.

# The Case of the Red Room

## The Case of the Red Room

"Oh, Doctor Watson, sir, you've come. Thank you ever so. Come upstairs, do."

"Mrs. Hudson," I said, "Whatever is the problem? Is he ill?"

"No sir, not as I can say exactly. But I don't like the look of him, that I don't."

I followed Mrs. Hudson up the familiar stairs. It has been some months since I had been back to the rooms at Baker Street, but as I ascended, it appeared that nothing had changed, including, perhaps, the fraught relations between my old friend, Holmes, and Mrs Hudson, our long-suffering landlady. She turned to me as we neared the top of the stairs.

"Oh, I do beg your pardon, Doctor. I did mean to ask you, how are you getting along? And Mrs. Watson? Is she well?"

"Thank you, Mrs. Hudson. We are getting along very well. My practice keeps me fairly well occupied and in fact Mrs. Watson is …well she is …perhaps I can say that we have just engaged an extra girl to do some of the heavier work"

"Oh, Dr. Watson, who'd have thought? I do congratulate you."

We had reached the top of the stairs. My eyes downcast, I saw how worn the landing carpet had become and I wondered whether it had always been thus or whether I was simply looking at it with fresh eyes. Mrs. Hudson stepped towards the parlour door and to my surprise, briskly opened it without a knock.

She stepped in and stood back for me to enter.

I took a pace inside and stopped, gazing at the room before me. This was the room I had seen in every conceivable state of disorder; from teetering stacks of undocketed papers on every surface, to Petrie dishes and Bunsen burners filling the atmosphere with putrid gases or malevolent miasmas; to rowdy Irregulars lounging noisily on the sofa and the armchairs, throwing boots, toast and anything within reach at each other, and all the while would be Holmes standing by the fire languidly holding the floor with his steely silence.

But the familiar room held none of that colourful charge. Holmes was there – I saw him at once – but this was not the Holmes of old. This was a languorous changeling, a pallid and threadbare presence on the sofa. He turned as I entered and fixed a pale gaze upon me. After several moments he spoke.

"Watson, I do believe. Watson. You are here. Thank you, Mrs. Hudson. Perhaps some tea."

Mrs. Hudson looked at me searchingly. I nodded gently to her and she withdrew.

"Holmes, old man." I began. "Look here, you're not quite yourself. Let me take a look at you. I have my bag." I brought it forward and began to open it, intending to bring forth my stethoscope.

"Watson, my old friend, you can take your bag with you to Hades. It is not medical attention I am in need of."

My hand stilled. "Holmes," I said. "What is it? What troubles you?"

He laid his head back and sighed. "Trouble. Yes, there is something in that. I am troubled indeed, though I doubt even your particular skills can assist me on this occasion."

"I say Holmes, old chap, you must tell me what ails you. You know I will do everything in my power to assist."

He sighed again, and I confess that the sound hollowed me. "Watson, I know precisely the progression of your thoughts. You see me somewhat ashen and shall we say, in a degree of lowered spirits. Your natural inference will be that I am not at present engaged upon a case." I nodded. Thus far his surmise was an obvious one.

"And you are then moved to speculate that I have succumbed to my evil familiar, who roosts upon my shoulder, hissing – unless that is a perhaps little too colourful – in my ear." Again, I nodded, but this time with downcast countenance. I knew too well the ravages called up by my old friend when he surrendered to the chemical authority.

"Ah, Watson. An understandable conclusion but not, this time, correct. I am without a case, it is true, but I have not as yet yielded to the hypodermic. The truth is a little more banal. I believe I have been suffering from what Shepherds Bush and its environs refer to as a 'bad oyster.'"

I barked a short laugh before biting it back. Holmes had a hangover. No medical attention required or of use.

"One too many, old boy?"

"Precisely. Not my finest hour. Mrs. Hudson may perhaps have witnessed some things rather beneath my usual dignity. She was naturally concerned. She sent for you. I thank you for presenting yourself."

I placed my bag on the floor and settled into the basket chair, chuckling. "This is not like you, Holmes. A little wine with dinner, a little cognac afterwards, but I don't believe I have ever seen you suffer in this way."

He shifted his weight and raised his arms above his head in an indolent stretch. "By all means amuse yourself at my expense, Watson. I believe I owe you that. However the moment Mrs. Hudson returns with that tea, if indeed she intends to do so in this lifetime, I mean to tell you rather an interesting tale that has begun to snake itself around me in recent days."

At that moment there was a tap at the door, and I rose to admit Mrs. Hudson bearing a heavy tray, which she set on the tea table. "There you are, Dr. Watson and Mr. Holmes: crumpets, toast, gooseberry jam, butter and of course the lapsang souchong." She glanced at Holmes and at me. I tilted my head and smiled. "Thank you, Mrs. Hudson, I believe we will do very well."

She smiled briefly as she left the room.

Holmes neatly pushed himself up to sit and took the cup I held out to him with a nod. "You must know," he began, "that my brother Mycroft sent me an urgent message two days since. You know of old that a message from Mycroft presages matters of the utmost national importance. It is impossible to overstate the critical nature of the questions exercising Mycroft's thoughts." Holmes sipped his tea and abstractedly reached for the crumpet I had buttered for myself.

"Yes, I said, for a moment watching the crumpet. "I am only too aware of the grave responsibilities he holds."

"And so it was in this case. He sought assistance with a practical matter, which his highly theoretical capacities did not equip him to manage himself, and discretion was vital. The problem was a moderately intriguing one, concerning two heads of state, of countries we generally consider to be friends, and some state secrets. Most intriguing. In fact, I rather regretted the necessity of my declining to assist Mycroft in the matter." Holmes took a dainty bite, and another, placing the crumpet on his saucer while he sipped his tea.

I waited, determined to resist the compulsion to ask him why. It was his tale: he could tell it. I buttered another crumpet and bit into it. My peripheral vision told me that Holmes shot me an amused glance. It was no good.

"Why?" I asked. "Why did you have to decline?"

Holmes paused for a moment, silently acknowledging to himself the point he had scored in the abstruse and solitary game in which he so often engaged. "Because, my dear fellow, I had just accepted another commission of a type which I did not envisage being able to execute simultaneously with Mycroft's."

"Another case? But I thought you said you did not have any engagement at present."

"That is so. I believe I dated Mycroft's proposal at two days since. The other little matter I had accepted earlier that same day. Ergo, my case-less state today implies that I have solved that matter at some point in the last two days, with the high probability of that successful culmination having been achieved subsequent to Mycroft's offer."

In spite of Holmes' irritating pedantry, I chuckled. "And observing your condition today, I believe it would be safe to hazard that this solution was reached prior to last night."

"Very good, Watson. Very good indeed. I would almost suggest your deductive reasoning had improved since your removal to your connubial domicile, if you had not, unfortunately, been quite wrong."

Dash the man. I took a hasty gulp of tea and bite of crumpet. "Very well, Holmes," I said curtly. "You have me at your service, and, as usual, at a disadvantage. Pray enlighten me."

"Forgive me, Watson. My condition has not, it seems, improved my civility. If you would do me the kindness to refill my cup, I believe I will just make myself comfortable with these cushions and tell you all I can about the two cases.

"Mycroft received my refusal with very bad grace. I believe he had not anticipated my being engaged, or at any event, my being disinclined to abandon whatever case in which I was currently enmeshed. I told him that I was not his assistant. He reminded me of my duty to my Queen and country, forgetting for the moment that this has never been as potent a call to me as that of the intriguing or obscure. Seeing his error, he then appealed to this very appetite, retelling the problem as though it were a perplexing mystery. Again, I refused. 'Damn it, Sherlock,' he finally said. 'I will make a bargain with you. If I solve your little problem, you will help me to solve mine.'

"To his astonishment, I not only held firm, but went so far as to counter his offer with one of my own: I would solve my problem without his assistance and then, if he were still in need of help, I would solve his."

Not for the first time, I was struck by the tendency of the brothers to vie against one another, and I tried unsuccessfully to imagine them as boys together. Echoing my thoughts, Holmes murmured, "It is almost as though he has not noticed the passage of time, and that I am not simply here to do his bidding. Am I the only practical recourse available to him?"

"Holmes," I said, "You forget that I remain in the dark. What was the case that held your interest so strongly?"

Holmes replaced his cup and closed his eyes, leaning back against the cushions. "My head pounds a little, Watson. You have your bag. I believe there will be something in it that would ameliorate my condition."

"No," I replied, not to be swayed. "Certainly not. Now, pray continue with your story."

"Ah well. The case," he mused. "The case began as usual with a message from a stranger. The Boots brought up a telegram, which proved to be from a distraught young gentleman who found himself in the custody of the police. The message said that he regretted that he had been unable to make an appointment to see me in my rooms, but that circumstances had got the better of him and he begged me to come to him immediately and with all haste."

"And who was this importunate fellow?"

"Reach behind you, Watson, and find yesterday's Times. Turn to page 11 and you will have your answer."

"Shipping tragedy, woman murdered, steel business collapse. I say, Holmes, what is it I am looking for?"

Holmes folded his fingers and closed his eyes again. "Young tutor released from custody."

I found the small item and read about an unusually named young Australian, Carig Stenborg, who held the position of tutor to the small son of the notorious actress Carmelina de Luca. It appeared he had been arrested two days ago for the theft of a valuable painting belonging to Miss de Luca, and then released within hours. There was a quote from our old friend Lestrade, who in his moralising way adjured the populace to keep strictly within the law whilst not actually providing any information about the case.

Holmes was closely following my reading of the article, and no doubt my expressions betrayed me, for he laughed outright as I folded the paper.

"Watson, Watson, you are as good as a comic turn."

I puffed out my cheeks and began to speak but he interrupted me.

"I saw your initial impatience as you searched for the story then your immediate but momentary puzzlement at his name – and incidentally, I agree with you: I believe it to be an invention. You then scowled your conservative anger at the name of Carmelina de Luca, and I believe the regret crossed your mind that I will persist in taking on the cases of our, shall I say, more colourful neighbours. And finally, your nostalgic warmth at seeing Lestrade's name was followed by a forgiving amusement at his empty bluster."

It was no good: I had to laugh with him. He was of course quite right in all respects. "But you know it to be true," I protested. You do your reputation no good by mixing with the demimonde. That woman is no better than a – "

"She is an actress, Watson. Let it rest there. And the case as presented to me by young Mr. Stenborg suggested some rather unusual details which rather piqued my interest. But look here, rather than listening to me tell the story, wouldn't you like to hear it from the gentleman himself? I rather fancy he is still reeling from the excitements of the past eight and forty hours and would be grateful for the opportunity to relate his tale to a new listener so that he might order the events in his mind. I am feeling much restored, and I had intended to visit him in any case, as there are one or two little developments about which he remains in ignorance."

"I should be most interested, but will he really see us?"

"I am certain of it. Mr. Stenborg was exceedingly grateful when I was able to unwind the tightening restraints that were beginning to augur so ill. Of course, it was a simple matter but not without its points of interest. And now that I am entirely fortified by tea and crumpets – thank you for allowing me to eat yours, by the way – I will send him a note suggesting that we meet at his place of employment in an hour."

Some little time later, as we walked through the thin light we Londoners choose to call sunshine, I reminded Holmes that he had promised to tell me about Mycroft's matter as well.

"Ah, yes," said Holmes. "Rather a dark tale of treason, I am afraid. A British spy, in fact, attempting to sell some secrets of the realm to an interested party or two." He then continued, more to himself than to me, I fancied, "But I can't simply drop my cases when Mycroft needs a more active pair of hands. Ah, here we are."

We had arrived at the entrance of the Oxford and Cambridge Mansions. The many fronted and rather imposing building held multiple apartments. We consulted a directory in the vestibule and took two flights of stairs to apartment 36. The door was opened by a timid young girl who, after a couple of ragged curtseys, showed us through to the drawing room.

Never had I seen such a vulgar room. The walls were papered in rich red flock and decorated with almost breathtakingly tasteless paintings in the pre-Raphaelite style: swooning, romantic, quite uncomfortable to behold. The carpet was deep crimson and the furniture plush and opulent. A tall, rather athletic young man stepped forward to greet us. He seemed at odds with his surroundings: neatly dressed, clean shaven and alert.

"So good of you to come, Mr. Holmes," he began, and I heard at once the painfully flattened vowels of the antipodean. "I must say that my head is still swimming. I can't make it out at all. And I have no idea where Miss de Luca is. There has been no message, yet her son is still here." He paused and collected himself, turning to me. "Forgive me, sir, you must be Dr. Watson. You are most welcome to my employer's home. Allow me to ring for some tea."

Holmes and I assured him we wanted no refreshment, and I believe I saw something like relief in his eyes. The status of a tutor can be an ambiguous one at best, and in such an outré household as he found himself, he might have been anticipating some difficulties with the kitchen. He ushered us to the sofa while he remained standing.

"As I understand it, Mr. Holmes, you would like to hear my story again."

"If you would be so kind," said Holmes. "There are one or two points that still puzzle me and the good Dr. Watson has not yet heard the tale."

"One or two points!" exclaimed Stenborg. "Why the whole chain of events mystifies me utterly. But then, that is why I sent for you when it happened. At any rate, thank goodness the picture has been returned." He dipped his head and smoothed his lapels in what appeared to be an effort to collect his thoughts, before turning to sit in a large armchair facing us.

"I am responsible for the education of Miss de Luca's son, Lorenzo," he began. "I must say that the word 'education' is perhaps a little hard to justify: The child is three years old." He opened his hands in an embarrassed but philosophical gesture. "I had settled the appointment by letter from home and the boy's age was never mentioned. I am afraid I was duped, rather. But once here, it was difficult to leave, and in fact the boy is so charming and warm-hearted, I quickly became fond of him and accustomed to my rather unusual situation."

"And Miss de Luca?" I asked.

He paused for a moment. "My salary is a good one, I have my own private apartment here and the duties are light." He paused again. "But I have not answered your question, Dr. Watson," he said frankly. "The truth is that my circumstances here are not something I have chosen to describe in my letters home. I have naturally become aware of Miss de Luca's reputation in society over the past few months, and frankly, I can't see my parents approving of my position. I rather think I would be summoned home on the next ship. But you see, I like it here." He cast his gaze around the garish room with something like appreciation and I almost felt myself shudder. "Perhaps it is easier for me to find myself comfortable in this … ambiguous situation than it might be for my English brethren. I'm sure you can imagine that growing up in the colonies of Australia and New Zealand was a rather rough and ready business, in spite of my time at university.

Miss de Luca treats me well – she is somewhat egalitarian, as am I – and we are on quite friendly, even warm, terms. There is often lively company of an exceedingly interesting and cosmopolitan type, and which on frequent occasions I am fortunate enough to be able to join. And of course, I am … flexible, shall we say, in my outlook and I make no judgements about how she chooses to lead her very independent life."

I cleared my throat and glanced at Holmes' expressionless profile. For once I felt I was reading his thoughts rather than he reading mine. This was no time for an offended outburst from me. I admit to being conservative and perhaps my views are old-fashioned, but clearly, they had no place here. "Thank you," I said quietly. "You have made yourself very clear."

Holmes gave the slightest of nods, and I felt a reluctant pleasure at having made the correct response. "Now, take us if you will to the afternoon of two days since,' he said.

Stenborg raised his hands in perplexity. "It was the strangest thing," he began. "I was home with Lorenzo, here in the drawing room. His nurse Bennet was in her room and Mrs. Greer the cook and Flynn the maid were in the kitchen. Miss de Luca was out. She had told me she was going to the theatre – it was the final night of her play, and she was going in early for some little celebration with the cast. Lorenzo and I were working at some drawing on the table here when I suddenly became aware of the sound of running water. I turned and looked at that wall." Here he indicated the wall in which the door was positioned, opposite the window. I looked with distaste at the gauche, rather tawdry painting hanging there, and realised that there was evidence of where water had run down the flocking. "It's all dried out now, of course," he said, "and it seemed safest to simply put the painting back once it was returned, but there was water flowing down the wall! Inside the room! So of course, I grabbed the Rossetti. Art is Miss de Luca's passion, as you can see, and that painting is her most important work."

I did my best to remain impassive at this outrageous remark; however, something in my demeanour gave me away. Stenborg faced me. "Dr. Watson, I can tell you that that painting is extremely valuable and is insured for a considerable sum."

"Very good," said Holmes. And then?"

"Well, I placed it safely against the opposite wall and rang for help. Flynn appeared and took Lorenzo up to Bennet while I sent an urgent message to Miss de Luca. Before long the water ceased to flow and within twenty minutes two men arrived from Sotherby's to collect the picture for safe keeping. Mrs. Greer summoned some extra help to clean up the carpet, and we lit a fire to help things to dry out, and I believed we had done all we could, though I still had no idea where the water had come from nor why it had stopped."

"And then?" asked Holmes again.

"Well then, I had just settled back to drawing with a rather excited Lorenzo when two police constables came to the door. In short, I was arrested for the theft of the painting and taken away to the West End police station, where you subsequently found me."

I gave a low whistle. Something in the young man's frank manner spoke of honesty, though the tale seemed bizarre. He certainly did not strike one as an art thief, and yet in my many adventures with Holmes over the years, I had, if nothing else, learned not to trust my own impressions, so I resolved to put them to the test.

"Now look here," I said. "The story you are asking us to believe is outlandish: a river running inside a house, an innocent man arrested. Surely at the very least you must have had some evidence of where the painting was being taken by the Sotheby's men, and could simply supply this information to the police?"

"That's just it," said Stenborg, ruefully shaking his head. "It never occurred to me that they were imposters. My feeling was relief that Miss de Luca had known exactly what to do when she received my note. Arranging for the painting to be immediately taken away to safety seemed so clever that I didn't think to ask the men anything nor seek any assurances from them. And after all, what was my authority to do so? And so this beautiful work of art simply went out the door and down the stairs." He turned to gaze at the picture in question with a vapid adoration. I twisted a little in discomfort. It was a florid and, to my mind, rather risqué than otherwise representation of a young girl in what appeared to be a state of abandon. I felt it was highly improper to be hanging on the walls of a family home, however unconventional the family.

"Now Watson," said Holmes, "you will have noticed the very curious circumstance here."

"Of course," I said, after a moment's thought. "Those crooks knew that word had been sent to Miss de Luca and timed their entry accordingly. In fact," and here I grew animated, "they must indeed have intercepted Mr. Stenborg's message to have known. Therefore, we can reason that if we find the messenger, we find our thief, and reclaim the painting!" I cried.

Silence greeted my brilliant deduction. Stenborg merely looked puzzled, and glanced again at the painting, quite real and hanging on a real wall.

Holmes, confound him, was vastly amused. It was clear that, not for the first time, I had set off down the wrong path altogether. My face flushed with mortification.

"First, my dear Watson, the painting does not at this moment appear to require reclaiming."

"No, of course it doesn't," I muttered.

"Second, while intercepting the note might at first blush seem shrewd on the part of the thieves, explain to me how they could have known there was a note, and even had they known, you will own that it would have been remarkably quick work for the crooks to concoct the plan and effect the disguises in the twenty minutes they had available. While the note and the arrival of the men occurred in sequence, there is no evidence to suggest a causal connection. On the contrary, I believe there is none. There are however two facts that *must* be connected: the removal of the painting and the flooding of the wall. If we take it that the object of our unknown culprit was to acquire this valuable painting, then our attention is drawn to any circumstance which might further this aim. Consider: under what circumstances would a member of this household stand by while strangers carry its most valuable object out through the door? I believe there are two possible answers: either its sale, which the household would certainly expect to be advised of, or its imminent danger. Ergo, the removal of the Rossetti followed the flooding of the walls, which was of course deliberate and targeted."

Stenborg made no response, and I surmised he had heard this theory from Holmes in their previous interaction. I, on the other hand, was all astonishment. "I simply don't understand," I burst out. "How does one flood the walls of someone else's house?"

"This is an apartment, is it not? And we are on the second floor of a building of how many floors? Four, precisely. So thus we know that there is a residence directly above us, a fact confirmed by the staircase we saw continuing up beyond this floor, and the register we consulted in the vestibule. Correct so far?" I nodded meekly and turned to Stenborg who followed Holmes' words expressionlessly. The familiar feeling of being inexorably drawn towards a petty humiliation began to suffuse me.

"Mr. Stenborg's supposition that the painting went out the door and down the stairs was a natural enough one in the circumstances: we unconsciously assume that leaving an apartment means exiting the street door. However, when I spoke to Stenborg in the police cell and learned of the two salient facts, the water and the theft, my attention of course turned to the floor above. Not only was it almost certainly the source of the water, but to retreat to it with the painting would provide immediate safety from observation, whereas carrying such a large and unusual object into the street would invite curiosity. Mr Stenborg, I believe you said that you did not follow the men to the door, nor actually observe them take the stairs down to the street? Quite so. Once my attention was thus focussed up rather than down, I sent for Lestrade, suggesting that he introduce himself to the tenants of the floor above and that he make sure to do so in the company of some hefty members of the constabulary. I advised him that he was looking for a very valuable work of art, some intriguing home plumbing that I rather fancy has not been approved by the building's owners, and a couple of solid individuals of the carrier class. I was not convinced that the coordinator of this strange little activity would also be at home, but I rather thought she might."

"She?" both Stenborg and I exclaimed.

"Indeed. I am sorry, Mr. Stenborg, that your comfortable situation as tutor must now come to an end, but I doubt Miss de Luca can continue to maintain this establishment from prison, where I have no doubt she will find herself. The official force can generally accomplish this much."

My surprise was as nothing to Stenborg's, and I was glad he was still seated. It is always a surprising thing to witness a vigorous young man succumb to shock, and indeed he swooned. His healthy colour drained instantly, and he weakly put his hand to his brow. As I rose to go to him, I glanced around the room and observed a decanter on a side table by the window. "Quick, Holmes, the brandy!"

Stenborg roused himself quickly after we handed him a tumbler of the stimulant and helped him to drink it.

"What you must think of me!" he said. "Oh," he groaned. "Good heavens – what will my mother say?"

"I shouldn't think your mother need become acquainted with all of the details of this little affair," observed Holmes. "And I offer you an apology. Like your employer, I sometimes favour the theatrical to a fault. I am afraid I did not consider your relationship with Miss de Luca when I made my revelation just now."

"Relationship?" I asked.

Stenborg rested his head against the back of the armchair. "It appears nothing escapes your powers, Mr. Holmes. It is true that on occasion Miss de Luca has found herself without an escort and has requested that I hand her in to dinner or accompany her to a recital. She has found my company acceptable: I believe she has appreciated the combination of youth and worldliness, not found so often in an Englishman of education. And I am not entirely naïve: I have also been aware that she loves to provoke the society that does not quite accept her, and being occasionally seen in public with an unranked member of her household staff gave her a certain frisson."

He said no more, though I had the very strong sensation that there might have been a great deal more to tell. I thought it wise to cover his discomfiture with speech. "So Miss de Luca was responsible for the entire subterfuge? And had access to the apartment above? To what end?"

"Ah, I believe it is the usual tired old reason, Watson. Miss de Luca's establishment is run on a comfortable scale, as you see, and I believe her personal expenses have not been modest, yet her income, tied as it is to her popularity, has necessarily been precarious. When such an uncertainty is coupled with a very strong desire to conquer in society, the conflict is inevitable. I learned from the distraught Mr. Stenborg, when I visited him in police custody, of the value of the painting and that it was heavily insured. One person emerged as the most likely gainer from this ingenious theft. I believe Miss de Luca hoped to retain the insurance money and then sell the painting itself to some unscrupulous collector, probably on the Continent. I dare say the transaction was already arranged. Thus a double return for her original purchase price, and I would even go further: I am willing to wager that the painting itself has not even been paid for."

Stenborg had recovered himself and hastily stood as a dawning understanding lit his countenance. "Lorenzo!" he cried. "The boy has been abandoned!" He rushed from the room and we heard him hasten along the passageway, calling out as he went. A few moments later he returned. "They have gone!" he said. "Bennet and Lorenzo, they are not there, and it looks as though they have taken away some belongings." He stepped to the hearth and rang the bell. "Reilly will know."

He rang again but there was no response. On investigation, we found the kitchen as deserted as the bedrooms. The child was gone, and the three women gone with him or scattered, recipients, apparently, of some hurried communication that might perhaps have included Stenborg himself had he not been ensconced with Holmes and me.

Stenborg was disconsolate. I watched him slump into the opulent armchair, a young man far from home, suddenly finding himself with no position and with his future prospects indelibly marred by an association with a notorious situation, and indeed I believed he was genuinely pained by the abrupt loss of two people for whom he cared. I couldn't help but hear his earlier cry reverberate in my mind: "The boy has been abandoned."

We brought Stenborg back to Baker Street, having taken care to lock the apartment carefully. The painting was now Lestrade's problem and I was pleased rather than otherwise to be leaving it behind. Mrs. Hudson provided us with an excellent supper, the hour for tea having long passed, and as we sat around the table after it was cleared, passing the decanter and the cigars, Holmes added some final details to our understanding.

"When I went to see Mr. Stenborg in the police cells and heard his story, I did not need to visit the apartment to realise what had transpired, and that Stenborg was obviously innocent of any crime," and here he turned to me with a smile, "notwithstanding any offences against good taste, of course. Lestrade was reluctant to release him on my authority alone, especially as he had received the complaint of the theft directly from Miss de Luca. However, I began to suspect what was afoot and was able to convince Mycroft to apply some influence to the Chief Constable. Stenborg was released, as reported in yesterday's paper, and Lestrade was sent to secure the painting and arrest the crooks. Unfortunately, Miss de Luca herself had flown, but her associates are now safely in our friend the Inspector's care.

"A propos of Mycroft, Watson, you will recall my mentioning him when we first spoke this morning. As it happens, I expect a new message from him imminently."

"Of course," I said. "You declined to help him in his matter. Do you anticipate his renewed appeal, especially now that he has helped you in your case?"

"On the contrary. I anticipate his gratitude. Rather than his helping me to resolve my little matter, I rather think I have resolved his." I exchanged a look of puzzlement with Stenborg, and at that moment there was a tap at the door and the Boots entered with a telegram in his hand.

"Please, sir, Mr. Holmes. This has come, sir." Holmes took the message from him and carried it to the lamp to read.

"Just so," he said to himself. He turned to the waiting Boots. "Please tell Mrs. Hudson my brother will be joining us immediately but we shan't require anything." The Boots left the room.

"Most unusual," I commented. "I don't believe I have seen Mycroft here more than once in a twelvemonth. I thought only the most important of matters warranted his personal attention."

"Indeed, that is so. As a matter of fact, this *is* rather an important matter. Ah, here we are." At that we heard a heavy tread ascend the stairs, followed by another slightly behind.

Stenborg stood hurriedly. "I say, what is all this? What the deuce is going on?"

Mycroft Holmes entered the room, looking deceptively genial and decidedly out of breath after climbing the stairs. He was if anything stouter than the last time I had seen him, and he dabbed a handkerchief across his glistening forehead as he spoke.

"Sherlock. Watson. May I?" he sat at the table next to Stenborg. "Stenborg, I believe?"

A uniformed constable entered the room, removing his hat and holding it quietly under his arm as he stood by the door.

"Worked with Miss de Luca?" went on Mycroft. "Not her real name of course. Not even Italian. Irish. O'Brien. But you weren't to know."

I shared Stenborg's utter astonishment as Mycroft continued. "Espionage, but not very good at it. Little too fond of the high life. None of it paid for. Made an unfortunate acquaintance or two. Rather think you might be able to help us out there. Believe you had some high old dinners? Foreign nobles. Household names. Might recognise some faces. Would you mind?"

Stenborg looked at Holmes, who smiled reassuringly. "Yes, it's perfectly all right. Mycroft will keep you safe and I dare say put you up for a week or two somewhere. You might be glad of a roof while you decide whether to take passage back to Australia or make another attempt to establish yourself in England." Holmes leaned towards him across the table. "I must say," he said confidentially, "most posts for tutors in this country are a little more conventional than your first experience has been. Much more respectable, but perhaps a little more work and a little less colour. However, I am sure we can find some suitable line of work for you."

Stenborg smiled ruefully and shook his head with bemusement. He turned to Mycroft as they both rose to leave. "I'm at your service, sir, and really, I rather think I can help."

After their departure, Holmes and I returned to the decanter and sat companionably.

"I say Holmes," I said, after a few minutes' reflection, "I believe you're up to something with Mycroft and young Stenborg."

Holmes reached for his briar and settled back in his armchair. "Indeed I am, Watson. You have hit upon it," said he, with quiet amusement. "Mycroft has unique abilities, as you know, but these unique abilities do not include any aptitude to work the ground, as it were. There are times when he requires some confidential and worldly, yet practical, assistance. He then calls upon me. But what if I am engaged, as occurred two days since, or indeed, not in the humour to accede? I came to the view that my dear brother, dweller in the abstract and arcane, required a pragmatic but cultivated amanuensis, and when in my first conversation with Stenborg I recognised some of the names from around Miss De Luca's table as being on Mycroft's own list, I began to see my way clear. I think that Mycroft's shadowy world of secret activity and rank might rather suit our broad minded young Australian friend. I daresay this won't prove to be a permanent arrangement, but I can confess to you, my dear Watson, that it does amuse me rather to gain a point over Mycroft."

I considered for a moment, warmed by his confidence, "And last night's revels?"

"Well," said Holmes, filling his pipe with tobacco, "unlike myself, Mycroft can be very stubborn. It required a little more application that I had anticipated to convince him of the value of employing an assistant. His cellar sustained some heavy losses, however as you saw, he had come around to my way of thinking."

"Of course he had. Well done, old chap." I rose, and picking up my hat, moved to the door. "I must be getting home to Mary."

"Do please give her my regards," said Holmes, "and I trust she will feel less uncomfortable shortly."

"How the …" I began, then thought better of it. "Goodnight Holmes."

"Good night Watson, old fellow."

# The Case of the Gold-Plated Aeroplane

## The Case of the Gold-Plated Aeroplane

I thought I heard the sound of a woman's voice as I made my way upstairs on the heels of the Boots.

"Oh," I said in some surprise, "Does Holmes have company?"

"Yes he does, sir, and doesn't she laugh? I should say she does."

"But who is it?"

"I'm sure I can't say, sir. It's another one. Only, Mrs. Hudson tells me specially not to disturb them. Which is all very well, but Mr. Holmes asked me to take in the sherry most particular. So bless me if I know am I going in or staying out. Then you knocked, sir, so I was off down again." He stood indecisively at the head of the stairs where I saw that a silver tray had been placed on the small side table by the drawing room door. On it were the sherry decanter, two of Mrs. Hudson's etched crystal glasses and a little dish of biscuits.

I paused as the Boots looked up at me. "What shall I do, sir?" he asked me.

"Well, well," I said, looking down at his little jacket. "Your buttons are wrong. You had best go and get them in order. I will take this matter into my own hands. Go on, then," I waved the boy away as he stood uncertainly for a moment before scampering off. At this moment I heard from within the drawing room the sound of a somewhat immoderate feminine laugh and thought that Boots' assessment had perhaps been accurate.

Holmes entertaining a lady in private was not a spectacle I was prepared to forego. Perhaps he had undergone an alteration in his estimation of the gentler sex since my recent removal. Perhaps indeed my own marriage had influenced him, though in truth it was difficult to imagine his softening on this question. I was aware that my scheme to intrude risked if not Holmes' ire then at least that of Mrs. Hudson. I took a breath, gave a quick double knock at thc drawing room door, and cntcrcd.

"Holmes," I said, "I was passing Baker Street on my way home and – oh I say, do forgive me. I had no idea you had company." I feigned surprise as I turned to the sofa and the woman who was carefully arranged there. I believed I saw the trace of annoyance in her expression as she glanced at Holmes who was leaning by the window seat. He pushed himself upright and advanced toward me with his hand outstretched.

"Watson, Watson," he said warmly. "This is indeed a delightful surprise. Your arrival is most opportune – allow me to present Mrs. Carmichael." With an indecipherable glint in his eye, he introduced me to the woman who was now self-consciously touching the back of her carefully arranged hair, and patting her gloves. She was a handsome woman of not past forty, expensively dressed yet with a restrained, I thought almost embarrassed, air.

"I am delighted to meet you, Mrs. Carmichael," I said, bending over her hand, "and I trust you will forgive my boorish intrusion." On learning my name, she preened a little and let out a small murmur of amusement. "Oh, Dr. Watson, I have just longed to meet you. I simply devour your stories. "

"And speaking of stories, Mrs. Carmichael has been telling me a most fascinating story about her brother." Holmes turned to her. "Perhaps if we allow my friend Watson to take a seat you would be so good as to continue?"

"Well I, that is, it is quite a confidential matter, Mr. Holmes. I had made certain to speak with you privately."

"Ah, yes, discretion is indeed most important in cases like these; however, I can personally assure you of Dr. Watson's tact. Watson, do take a seat. I believe the basket chair will accommodate you admirably as of old."

I lowered myself into the familiar seat, puzzled by Holmes' curiously glib and careless manner.

Mrs. Carmichael looked doubtfully at Holmes, who nodded blandly at her and said, "Pray continue. I believe your brother, the vicar at St Anselm's, was it? had just experienced his second disturbance." Holmes turned to me and added confidentially,

"The unfortunate gentleman has to date received an anonymous note threatening his cabbages and some suspicious paint on his cucumber frames."

There was silence for a moment as Mrs. Carmichael looked steadily at Holmes. "Mr. Holmes," she said with a quaver, "I do believe you are laughing at me."

Holmes turned to the window, and pulling the curtain aside, murmured, "Another grimy night in London, it seems. Evening falls swiftly and night brings few diversions." He turned resolutely back to the room. "I offer you my profoundest apologies, Mrs. Carmichael. I am all contrition. I regret that you have found me in one of the ill humours that render me incapable of normal discourse. However, if it may be some recompense, I do not believe your brother to be in any danger and he does not require my assistance. I am quite sure that if he has a private interview with his curate, the mystery will be resolved without impact on his congregation."

"His curate?"

"Yes, a small matter of local competition, I believe. I hazard that the curate is also a vegetable gardener?"

She nodded, puzzled, her face pale.

"And many of his near neighbours, I don't doubt. However, my experience suggests that the closer the rivalry, the fiercer the retaliation. I am confident that the murky realms of local parish subterfuge are no exception to this universal law. If we then consider that the systems of ascending the church's hierarchy are piecemeal at best, the clerical factotum begins to emerge as a likely culprit. Mrs. Carmichael, I trust you will forgive me for making the observation that you have clearly been raised with a genteel hand."

At this, the woman's expression combined a simper with the surprise at Holmes's sudden change of direction.

"I am certain the same can be said of your brother. Thus we have privilege, position and prospects – "

"And cucumber frames?" I asked, impulsively.

"And indeed cucumber frames, inflaming the ambitious heart of the overlooked."

"The curate?" I was enjoying myself, in spite of Mrs. Carmichael's evident discomfort.

"The curate. And there we have it," said Holmes, moving forward and extending his hand, leaving Mrs. Carmichael no choice but to rise and, in some confusion, take her leave.

At the sound of the street door closing on her, Holmes flung his hands in the air with a loud grunt. "I blame you, Watson. For heaven's sake, pour me a sherry!" He threw himself onto the sofa with a deep frown as, somewhat bewildered, I fetched the tray from outside the door and poured two glasses, handing him one.

"I say, Holmes," I said tentatively. "What on Earth is it that you blame me for?"

"These women! That was the third in scarcely a week and that wretched Mrs. Hudson conspires; I know she does."

I was standing in the middle of the room, confounded, with my glass untasted in my hand. Holmes looked up and studied my uncomprehending face. "The stories, Watson, the stories. Your little accounts of our cases. These women," he all but spat the word, and tossed down most of the glass of sherry, "these women read them and then they come calling on me with their banal tales of, of …"

"Cucumber frames?" I hazarded.

He let out a roar and almost gnashed his teeth. "They simper, Watson. They laugh at nothing. They gaze at me. Oh, how they gaze! I have given the Boots multiple shillings to mislead lone females at the door, but Mrs. Hudson appears to have preternatural powers and won't see them turned away. Once installed, they are almost impossible to dislodge. I was much relieved when I saw your arrival through the window."

I chuckled. "It seems I have inadvertently created a phenomenon. I give you my word, old chap, it was never my intention to bring you an unwanted celebrity."

"Well it must cease. No more tale telling, Watson. It is insupportable." He strode to the hearth and rang the bell. I stood in some perplexity. Naturally I could see Holmes' position, but my view remained that some carefully curated accounts of Holmes' masterful talents were more than simply amusing to the public: They were instructive, and furthermore, I had a firm belief they represented a deterrent to the criminal classes.

"Now look here, Holmes. You can't ask me to stop presenting these tales."

He remained silent, staring at the hearthrug. There was a hesitant tap at the door, and it opened, revealing a reluctant Boots.

Holmes barked, "Fetch Mrs. Hudson, if you would be so good."

The boy hesitated. "Am I in trouble, sir?"

Holmes looked at him for a fleeting moment. "I believe you do your best in a sometimes conflicted circumstance."

After a moment of puzzlement, the boy's face lit up and he ducked from view. Shortly thereafter Mrs. Hudson joined us. She was clearly aware that Holmes was displeased, and she twisted her fingers together as she stood by the door.

"You wished to see me, sir?"

"Indeed, Mrs. Hudson, and this fact alone sets you very distinctly apart from all other members of your sex."

"Oh, I say Holmes," I interrupted. "You mustn't speak so. Not quite the thing, old man."

"Watson," he almost snarled, "pray do not 'old man' me, and allow me a little tete-a-tete with my landlady, if you would be so kind."

At this I subsided. "Mrs. Hudson," he continued, "I believe you are aware that there has been a recent increase in the number of women calling upon me. You are also aware that their frivolous, time-wasting and demeaning concerns do not constitute cases. You must understand that a woman is incapable of bringing me anything that will pique my curiosity. She possesses neither the subtlety nor the objectivity to do so. Do not delude yourself: I know you and your intentions full well, but I can assure you that I will not succumb to the charms of any one of these females. There will be no …" he sneered, "lovemaking, in your drawing room and there will be no Mrs. Holmes. Do I make myself clear?"

The room was silent but for the sounds of Holmes' harsh breathing through his dilated nostrils. I held my tongue, and Mrs. Hudson studied the floor. Finally, she murmured, "Very good, Mr. Holmes." At this, she paused, then raised her head with a defiant lift of her chin. "But I can only hope you're easy in your mind, sir, to speak in this way to a lady and a widow. I am sure I have done my best through trying circumstances, Mr. Holmes, and you will allow I have been slow to complain, even with pistols and poisons and disreputable types at all hours. You say you know me, sir, but I can say I know you. You are an arrogant and sarcastic man, Mr. Holmes, and clever as you be, you have no grace about you. The charm is there, sir, we all see it. But that's a hollow sort of thing to my mind. Now Dr. Watson here, he's a gent. You might do worse than to pattern yourself on Dr. Watson."

At this I rose, in some confusion and consternation. "Now look here," I began, "this is none of mine. I beg to be left out of this."

Holmes waved me back down. "Mrs. Hudson has the floor, I believe Watson."

"And as for what you say about ladies, Mr. Holmes, your mother would be ashamed of you I am sure. You sweep us all into one basket, the wicked with the good, the schemers with the angels, the clever with the daft, the poor soul from the street along with the innocent. Mr. Holmes, you do not like women and that is the truth, and while it grieves me to say you are not the only man so afflicted, I tell you now it's not women's fault, it's yours. And if you decide that you would prefer not to reside with a woman, I will accept your decision." At this, Mrs. Hudson quitted the room.

Holmes gave a low whistle and turned to the window, once again drawing the curtain back and gazing out into the dark street below. I shifted uneasily in the basket chair and recrossed my legs. Eventually I spoke.

"Look here, Holmes. You mustn't mind about all this. It's just Mrs. Hudson."

"I rather thought Mrs. Hudson felt she was speaking on behalf of her entire sex."

"Well, she, that is – "

"I am turning this over in my mind, Watson. A little earlier I instructed you to cease writing your stories because of their effect upon women. Now Mrs. Hudson accuses me of a sweeping prejudice against the fair sex. I shall tell you what I propose. If the next worthy case that comes to me is brought by a woman, you are free to continue your scribblings and I will be bound to make an apology to the good Mrs. Hudson."

"But this is mere chance, Holmes. One does not make wise decisions based upon chance."

"Does not one? Well, I am about to do so." He went to the hearth and began to fill his pipe from the Persian slipper. "And now let us see what fate has in mind for us. Perhaps there is a little amusement to be had after all."

Of course, no case came to Holmes that night, nor the next day. However, that following evening as I was finishing with my last patient, Mary, my wife, brought a telegram to me in the surgery.

"It's from Holmes," I said, thanking her with a kiss.

"Well, if he needs you, he's welcome," she said smiling. "The old bear would do well to pattern himself on a real gent." We laughed. I had of course told her of the previous evening's interesting events, and at my description of Mrs. Hudson's declaration, Mary's mirth was as immoderate as Mrs. Carmichael's had been. She read over my shoulder as I opened the message. "Come at once stop Mycroft sends a case tonight".

"I will make a sandwich," called Mary over her shoulder to me as she hurried away. "You shall make a gentleman of him yet!"

A short time later, I sat with Holmes over a glass of brandy as we waited for word from Mycroft. "Do you suppose he will come himself?" I asked.

"I shouldn't think so. You will recall that Mycroft has brought me a case on only three occasions, the most recent of which I declined."

"Ah yes," I replied. "In the case of that Australian fellow, Stenborg. I say, does that young chap still work for Mycroft?"

"I believe he does," replied Holmes. "However, I rather think that he is gradually disappearing into the shadowy world of international espionage and is well on the way to losing his identity all together."

"Good heavens, Holmes. This sounds grim."

"Not at all, Watson. I hazard that he is in his element – the game, the excitement, the danger – though I imagine his letters home to mother are somewhat circumspect. Ah! There is the street door. Our case presents itself."

We rose to greet our visitor. There was a tap at the door and the Boots entered. "Mrs. Pankhurst to see you sir."

I almost chuckled to see Holmes so discomposed. As a rule, impossible to fluster, he was nevertheless a trifle disconcerted as he greeted our visitor, made introductions and arranged our seating.

"The first thing I must say, Mr. Holmes," began Mrs. Pankhurst, "is that the trouble I bring to you is not in any way connected with my more public undertakings."

"Thank you, Mrs Pankhurst, I will bear that in mind, however I am sure you will allow me to withhold my judgement on that question until I am better acquainted with the particulars. Of course, I may say that you need no introduction: your works on behalf of your sex are well known to Dr. Watson and myself."

She gave us both a fresh, warm smile. "I won't ask your views on the question of universal suffrage, Mr. Holmes. I find that nothing cools a conversation more quickly. I am quite sure we can contain ourselves to the business at hand, upon which I sincerely hope you can shed some light." She pinched the fingers of her gloves and removed them, neatly placing them on her lap. "You will forgive me, I hope," she said, slightly raising her bare hands in explanation. "I find them so restrictive." And indeed, her hands were pleasantly expressive as she told her story.

"I had been busy in London for some months, Mr. Holmes, and the trials I had been facing had left me somewhat weary, when my husband, Richard, suggested we make a short visit to my sister's home in Dorset. I am the eldest of five girls, and Diana and I, though not the nearest in age, have always been very close. Since our move to London some ten years ago and then her recent marriage, I have seen little of her. But perhaps I am offering you unnecessary detail, Mr. Holmes. I should not like to waste your time, upon which I am sure many calls are made."

"Not at all, Mrs. Pankhurst. Your narrative is most succinct. Pray proceed."

"Thank you, Mr. Holmes. Very well: we arrived at Diana's home late in the evening about two weeks since, to find the house in some confusion. The domestics were nowhere to be seen – we later discovered they had been keeping to the kitchen – and my sister at first refused to see us. We were their guests yet had received no sort of welcome."

"Your sister's husband?" asked Holmes.

"Ah, indeed. My sister's husband. Mr. Jerome Firbank is the vicar of the parish where Diana makes her home and she does indeed have her hands full as the local clergyman's helpmeet. They live in the vicarage of course, and it is a little out of the way of the village. At any rate, Richard and I waited in the library for nigh on half an hour before we saw any signs of our hosts. Finally, Diana appeared at the door, looking fearfully at us from behind her hair, which was all down, and with an ashen face. Without speaking a word, she slipped into the library and closed the door behind her.

" 'Have you seen Mr. Firbank?' she asked us in a whisper. This is what she calls her husband, and many is the time I have remonstrated with her about this ludicrous and old fashioned formality between husband and wife. Be that as it may, she appeared to be in some distress, and we were naturally concerned.

" 'What is it?' I asked her. 'Diana, what troubles you? How can we aid you?'

"At this she burst into tears and cried that she feared for her husband's safety. He had left some hours previously to visit a row of nearby cottages on foot. There had been some illness amongst the tenants and Jerome is conscientious in the extreme about executing his parish duties. However, he had still not returned, and Diana had allowed herself to become consumed by some rather hysterical thinking. She was always a sensitive child, Mr. Holmes, and when she married the stern Mr. Firbank, who was many years her senior, I hoped that their match would be a more sympathetic one than it seemed to promise.

"I assisted her to bed immediately and called for some tea and for the fire in her room to be mended. As I helped her into her night things, I noticed that her arms were bruised. When I asked her about the marks, she snatched her arms away and refused to speak. At this I felt a chill. 'Is this Jerome's work?' I asked her, perhaps rather too harshly, for she hurried me from the room and locked her door.

"Richard and I made the best of our rather disquieting situation, settled into our room and made shift with some bread and cheese for supper, which we found for ourselves in the now deserted kitchen." Mrs. Pankhurst paused for a moment and looked enquiringly at Holmes. "I trust I am making myself plain, Mr. Holmes. Am I perhaps too prolix?"

"Not at all. I am all attention. Pray continue."

"The following morning Richard and I came down expecting to see both Jerome and Diana for breakfast, but neither was there, and the parlour maid was excessively nervous and silent. After breakfast I chased Diana down to her own room and found that she was still in bed, keeping in the dark and refusing to see anyone. I am afraid I forced my way in, Mr. Holmes. I have a personal creed, 'deeds not words,' and Richard will tell you that I will often find myself in difficult situations because of my somewhat impulsive nature. However, on this occasion I had every reason to thank the fates that blessed me with that nature for I found that the reason my sister was hiding was that she bore the marks of violence upon her face. One eye had closed entirely, and the flesh of her cheek was swollen and beginning to darken. In vain she attempted to conceal the injury from me, and in vain she entreated me not to rush to judgment. She claimed she had stumbled in the night and fallen against the bedstead. She was by now sobbing and close to collapse.

"Mr. Holmes, I must tell you that at the sight of my dear sister so ill-treated, my anger rose to quite a pitch. Richard was hard-pressed to contain me and to oblige me to see sense. Our first task, he rightly reasoned, would be to secure some confidential medical assistance for Diana. Our second would be to locate Jerome. Once we had achieved this, we might then ascertain whether our course of action would be to remove Diana immediately. In short, Mr. Holmes, we needed to know whether Jerome was the author of this unhappy situation."

"And did you find the missing Mr. Firbank?"

Mrs. Pankhurst sighed and adjusted her cuffs. "We did. He appeared some hours later, exhausted after having spent the night tending to the spiritual needs of one of his parishioners who was apparently facing a crisis. Jerome was most certainly not responsible for the injury to Diana's face. I confess that I checked his account with the servants who confirmed that he had not been home all night. I was suspicious, Mr. Holmes, but I fear that I was prejudiced by the fact that I do not like the man, and I was heartily ashamed to realise that I was acting outside a rational assessment of the circumstances." She again looked to her cuffs, and I stole a glance at Holmes. He was considering her words. There was a faint lift to his eyebrows as though to concede that Mrs. Pankhurst had gained a point. I was amused to note that her words, her analysis, could almost have been his own.

I leaned forward. "Did you succeed in finding some medical attention for your sister?" I asked.

"Yes, Dr. Watson, we did, and here my tale takes another turn. A local man was able to attend my sister within an hour. He examined her, much against her will but absolutely at my insistence. He established that the insult to her eye had probably occurred as the result of a fall, as Diana had maintained. I regretted profoundly that I had not believed her. My prejudice influenced my reasoning."

"And the bruising to her arms?"

Mrs. Pankhurst did not immediately answer my question. She bowed her head as though collecting her thoughts, again toying with her gloves, and then raised her head to face me directly. "The medical man who attended my sister, Dr. Watson, was of the opinion that the bruising, which was unfortunately more widespread than I had appreciated, was the result not of violence but of illness. He stated his view, in fact, that Diana is suffering from liver disease." Her gaze was steady, and I could well believe that it cost her dearly to maintain such calm.

"I see," I said slowly. "It is indeed the case that some diseases of the liver can cause such marks to appear upon the skin. And did he explain to you what was, in all likelihood, the cause of this condition?"

She lowered her gaze. "Yes, Dr. Watson, as I believe you have surmised, it transpires that my sister … takes a little too much wine, and has done for some time. She was in tears as she explained herself to us. It seems that her marriage is without joy. It has never given her the loving and spiritual happiness she had unquestioningly anticipated. I am afraid that with our own parents' mutual fondness, and then my own union with Richard, as models, she had foolishly believed that when one marries, one falls into a natural and inevitable state of connubial bliss, where one loves, enjoys and honours freely. The bitter truth is that they are an ill matched pair and have not brought each other mutual fulfilment. In addition to this personal disappointment, she has found her parish duties to be trivial, exhausting and lonely. Ultimately, in her misery, she found herself taking solace where she might. It seems that her constitution is weak, and she has fallen into a serious illness. Fate has indeed punished her cruelly, Mr. Holmes, Dr. Watson. She is now very ill. Richard and I brought her to London with us and have placed her in the care of an excellent nursing home very near to where we live in Russell Square."

"A difficult story to relate, I am sure," said Holmes thoughtfully. "Yet, Mrs. Pankhurst, I am still at a loss to understand what help you seek from me. What is it that I can do for you?"

She sighed sorrowfully. "It is Jerome. There is something amiss, but I cannot make it out. I have a foreboding sense that there is something very wrong, possibly dangerous, perhaps unconnected with my sister, and that I must act. But what it is that I must do, I know not."

I waited for Holmes' inevitable objection and brusque dismissal, for I well knew his disdain for anything that might be thought of as intuition, wedded as he was to the objective and the measurable. It was exceedingly puzzling for me, therefore, to see him pause and consider her words carefully and courteously, nodding in assent.

"Certainly, what an intelligent mind experiences as foreboding," he said, "is often the result of one's unconscious mind processing the facts that our conscious mind has not apprehended. I myself often act upon what might be called instinct, but what is in reality merely a heightened assessment of the evidence, a higher order of data processing, if you will."

I was astonished. Holmes had never once laid himself bare to me in this way. He had always been at pains to assert that he never acted on anything other than an intellectual analysis of the facts. I watched in wonder as he met Mrs. Pankhurst's eye with a steady and thoughtful gaze.

"It was Mycroft who sent you to me, I believe?" he asked.

At this, her face lightened. "Oh yes, Mycroft and I are quite old friends. He has been a material support in my work with the suffrage movement and shows a keen interest in the status that we women are beginning to claim." Holmes and I exchanged a slow look of wonder at this, a look that did not go unnoticed by the alert Mrs. Pankhurst. She smiled. "I see you are surprised, gentlemen. And yet surely, we are all somewhat of a closed book to those closest to us. I assure you that it is true: your brother exerts himself in our cause, and I find his influence to be extraordinarily far reaching. When I told Mycroft about my disquiet concerning my sister, he suggested I bring it here but made no comment other than to give me a message for you."

"A message?"

"Yes, Mr. Holmes. Mycroft told me that you would consider this a challenge: 'remember that the word 'resolve' has two meanings'. I almost wondered whether he knew something about the situation that he was not able to relate to me. Perhaps he believed that you could arrive at the truth yourself without his compromising privileged information."

Holmes held his chin reflectively. "I am in the humour to accept the challenge." He turned briskly to me. "It seems that a visit to Dorset is in order, Watson. Be so good as to check the Bradshaw. You'll find it there behind you, under those cuttings. I expect there to be a train leaving for the county after breakfast, and perhaps you could suggest to your good lady wife that she might do without you for an evening or so."

And so it was arranged: Holmes and I would leave for Dorset on the morrow, and Mrs. Pankhurst would remain in London. As we descended the stairs to the street door, she said, "You can't think how grateful I am, Dr. Watson, that you and Mr. Holmes will look into my concerns. I am only too conscious of the fact that I have no concrete evidence or information to offer, and nothing has really happened out of the ordinary. I really expected Mr. Holmes to dismiss my request out of hand. I believe Mycroft's word has carried some weight with him."

"That is in all likelihood true, but I confess that Mr. Holmes' decisions about whether or not to accept a case seem often to depend upon factors that only he can perceive. Perhaps it is what he called intuition just now." I opened the door for her, and we stepped out onto the street. She declined my offer to secure a cab for her, declaring her preference to walk the short distance. "At least let me accompany you," I said.

"By no means," she replied. "I am very comfortable walking alone. Good night, Dr. Watson, and thank you."

"Good night, Mrs. Pankhurst." For a moment I watched her walking briskly and confidently away, then I turned towards home.

I breakfasted with Holmes at Baker Street before we made our way by cab to Paddington. "No bag?" asked Holmes.

"Old campaigner and all that," I replied, "But I did think to bring my service revolver."

"I do hope that won't become necessary, but perhaps it is all to the good. I have my cane, as you see." He indicated his sword stick. "I rather fancy that there is something to this Firbank character, and my curiosity is piqued by Mycroft's referral to me. Perhaps there is nothing in it, but a trip to the Dorset Downs – ah, here we are at the station. I see we are in good time."

Our train journey was uneventful. Even the talkative elderly gentleman who shared our carriage for the first hour failed to provide amusement to Holmes, who steadfastly watched the changing landscapes through the window in silence.

Our stop was little more than a halt a few miles short of Dorchester and we were the only passengers to alight. After the guard had flagged the train onward, we enquired of him for directions to the vicarage and shortly found ourselves at the arboured gate of a pleasant old garden. A modest plate reading "Vicarage – J. M. Firbank" indicated a short gravel walk to what appeared to be the parish door. Our knock was answered by a somewhat lugubrious butler wearing a rusty black suit. He led us through to a faded parlour and withdrew.

I stood uncertainly by the hearth and turned to Holmes. "I say, Holmes, what do you mean to say to the man?"

Holmes calmly inspected the ornaments ranged across the sideboard – a small train, a model yacht – they looked like children's toys. "I? Oh, I shall say nothing. You, on the other hand –"

At this moment the butler returned followed by our host, or perhaps I should say, our quarry. Firbank was a thin, erect man bearing none of the signs of a peaceful bucolic life. His complexion was sallow and his countenance stern. His eye, which turned naturally to Holmes, was sharp and suspicious.

"To what do I owe this honour, gentlemen?" he asked, as the butler withdrew.

Holmes glanced at me with one eyebrow raised.

"Mr. Firbank," I began, and hesitated. "Mr. Firbank –"

"Perhaps I could suggest that we start with some names," he interrupted tersely. "After all, you have the advantage of me."

We introduced ourselves, whereupon Firbank immediately became more genial. "Ah yes," he said. "I had forgotten. My sister-in-law Emmeline mentioned your names to me in her letter overnight. You are here to gather a little more information about my wife and her unfortunate condition. Gentlemen, pray be seated and tell me what you wish to know."

Our interview with Firbank was a curious one. I felt that I was creeping forward in the dark, trying to guess what Holmes wished me to ask, what Mrs. Pankhurst had written to Firbank, and what facts he might be attempting to obfuscate.

Finally, after a few weak exchanges, he said, "Dr. Watson, perhaps it will help if I am completely frank with you. I must tell you that my wife," here he sighed deeply. "My wife is not … a happy woman. I believe her unhappiness to be a factor in her illness. I would go further and say that I am responsible. In fact, I regret marrying her. Not, I hasten to add, because I am not fond of her – I am very fond of her in my way – but because I wronged her in taking her so young from her comfortable family circumstances. I believe I may have been seduced by the idea of a happy home such as the Goulden family enjoyed and I was certainly intoxicated by the idea of what a strong presence like Emmaline's might bring to my humble parish. My mistake, for mistake it certainly was, had been to assume that Diana was simply a younger version of her older sister. I failed to observe her, Dr. Watson. I was blind to the fact that women are not all of a piece. My own circumstances have been somewhat sheltered, I am afraid, and I had the hubris to believe that my position gave me some sort of understanding unavailable to others." He remained silent for a while, his hands turning slowly over, and his head slightly bowed.

"Go on," I said gently.

He looked up at me. "Dr. Watson," he said, "I believe that God intends us each for a particular life, but that human weaknesses and failings sometimes derail our paths. My fancy is that I am like a train," his eyebrows indicated the model on the sideboard, "intended by God to stick to the known path and to apply myself industriously to his works. My folly was to assume that Diana would simply join with me in this labour. I now see that our maker never meant Diana for such dull endeavour." He lifted his face as though looking to the heavens. "She is somehow of the air, more like one of these lighter-than-air crafts than a mere train. An aeroplane, Dr. Watson. An aerial, luminous craft, gold plated almost." He dropped his gaze and sighed heavily. "And my blindness, my obstinacy, has left her earthbound. If I could free her of my ties, I would, but regrettably that is not possible."

As we sat in silence, there was a knock at the door. The butler quietly handed Firbank a telegram on a salver. Firbank opened it, glanced at it, and said "No reply," upon which the butler withdrew.

“It is a message from Diana, gentleman, requesting that I come to London to see her. If you will excuse me? There is much to see to.” We rose, and Firbank hastened from the room.

There was a London train an hour hence and we three took it together. Holmes and I smoked companionably, and Firbank sat meditatively in a corner of the carriage. On our arrival at Paddington, we made our farewells and he hurried away to see his wife. Holmes and I strolled back to Baker Street.

“Well, Holmes,” I said. “Rather a curious case, in that there was no case at all. I wonder what possessed Mycroft to send Mrs. Pankhurst to you on such a fool’s errand.”

“Fool’s errand, you say? You know of old that Mycroft goes devilish deep. I believe he had some sort of plan to, shall we say, enlighten me, and that Mrs. Pankhurst was the very apt tool to hand.”

“Do you mean to say that he knew there was not something amiss with Firbank?”

“On the contrary, I believe that Mycroft listened to Mrs Pankhurst’s story, surmised that the real issue was simply the misalliance between the two unhappy Firbanks, and then, Watson, the putative head of my family had the audacity to decide that this was the moment to teach me a brotherly lesson. He knew that his own name being brought to me by an articulate and sensible individual like Mrs Pankhurst, not to mention the cause she is associated with in the public mind, would be a temptation, or to use his own term, challenge, I could not resist."

"Good Heavens, Holmes," said I. "I had forgotten that challenge. Resolve, was it? What the devil did he mean by saying the word has two meanings?"

"Mycroft in his wisdom views my consulting work as somewhat mechanical. I wait for a problem to present itself, I solve it, I await the next problem. Indeed, he has more than once chided me with this rather superficial understanding of my work. If I interpret his message correctly, he is urging me to look beyond, to determine to be something more. In short, to *show* some resolve, rather than just *resolve* my cases. I fancy he saw there *had* been something amiss with our clerical friend, and that it was the same malady that Mycroft believes me to have been suffering from, and coincidentally, as does Mrs. Hudson and perhaps even you as well."

I thought this through for a moment, gradually beginning to see some light. "What, women?

"Yes, Watson, women. I have been bested. I was wrong. And now prepare yourself to see me humbled before Mrs. Hudson, oh and sharpen that pencil of yours. Your eager public awaits."

# The Case of the Tethered Goat

## The Case of the Tethered Goat

I thanked heaven for the deep gloom of evening when I knocked on the street door of Holmes' lodgings, but try as I might to hide my face in shadow, it was to no avail.

"Dr. Watson, sir!" said the sharp-eyed young Boots as he opened the door. "Whatever has happened to your face? You're black and blue!"

He hustled me inside and upstairs, though my ascent was painfully crabbed, and once we gained the landing, he opened the drawing room door without ceremony.

"Mr. Holmes, sir!" he said. "Dr. Watson has been injured. Lend a hand if you please, sir."

Holmes lay in his customary lounging position, stretched upon the settee with one long arm flung behind his head, an evil-smelling pipe smouldering in the other and one long leg hooked over the antimacassar.

"Well, well, my dear Watson," he said languidly, without displaying more movement than the slightest turn of his head. "It appears that this time it is the doctor who requires the doctoring. Whatever have you been up to, amusing yourself in this eccentric way?"

For a brief moment, irritation wrestled in my breast with relief to find my friend at home. The pain in my arm was now intense and I was coming to the realisation that my clavicle was fractured. The black eye was uncomfortable, the split lip soaking with blood the handkerchief I pressed to it, but the pain in my shoulder was penetrating my very senses.

"Footpads!" I exclaimed. "Just off the high street. I was set upon."

I collapsed into an armchair with a groan. At this, Holmes leapt up, tossing his pipe towards the hearth, and issuing a rapid instruction to the Boots to fetch a doctor, "and make haste!" he cried. "This instant!" The gaping boy scrambled back through the door and Holmes knelt at my side.

"Fool that I was," he said. "I was amused at your having a black eye, but I see that in truth you are hurt, my old friend. Your arm?"

"My shoulder. I believe it is broken. They had a truncheon."

Holmes paused at this. "And who were 'they'? What did they say?"

"There were three of them. They followed me into Brussells Lane – I was taking the short cut – and I thought nothing of it, the streets being quite busy at the beginning of the evening. But one of the scoundrels darted around in front of me and stood there, barring my way. Before I could ask him to move, the other two fellows came up behind. The first man called me by name and asked me for the documents."

Holmes rocked back on his heels, a look of hardness in his narrowing eyes. "Did they indeed?"

"Yes. I said I had none, and what did they mean and so on. I say, Holmes, I think I might just continue my exposition later. My arm is dashed uncomfortable."

Holmes was all contrition, and by the time he had fetched me a brandy and summoned Mrs. Hudson to hover, the Boots reappeared with Mackenzie, my medical colleague, hard on his heels.

While Mackenzie was confirming my pessimistic diagnosis of a broken bone, Mrs. Hudson took my instructions for a message to be sent to Mary. "She's in Liverpool for the week," I said. "She needn't come home – she has her work to do, and after all, what could she do for me here? Just write that I will be staying with Holmes for a bit." I reflected for a moment. Mary was perceptiveness itself: Nothing would bring her home more quickly that a vague message in someone else's hand. A telegram perhaps? No, that would raise an even more immediate alarm.

"On second thoughts, Mrs. Hudson, I am afraid I shall brook your disapproval and not send Mary any message at all."

"Dr. Watson, you must. Pray put yourself in that poor girl's shoes. She may be busy with her good works, but how will she feel when she learns of your injuries? And then, with not a soul letting her know, what will she think of me, I should like to know? Really, doctor, I should not have thought this of you."

At this point, Mackenzie began to bind my arm and shoulder, and, apologising to the good Mrs. Hudson, I waved her away with my left arm. She quitted the room, mussitating about supper. Mackenzie meanwhile wasted little breath on bedside reassurances. "You don't need me to give you the drill," he said, in a tone that was to my ear somewhat unsympathetic. He then commenced rummaging in his bag, muttering.

"Whatever now?" I asked peevishly. "Not much more you can do, old boy."

He held aloft an ampoule and a syringe case. "That's where you err, John. You won't get a wink tonight without some assistance."

I submitted to his injection of morphine, somewhat amused by the envious glint I detected in Holmes' eye.

In an increasingly drowsy state, I sat by the fire, Mackenzie on one side of me and Holmes on the other, prepared to tell the dramatic tale of my attack. The morphine, however, began to influence my recollection as well as my ability to articulate it. I became aware that the two of them found my halting speech, and increasing pauses, somewhat entertaining. The warm room seemed to throb pleasantly, the pain in my shoulder ebbed and I was suffused with an agreeable glow of comfort. How delightful it was to sit with two friends by a warm fire, another glass of brandy at hand and the prospect of a nourishing supper to be brought up to me betimes. However, when the supper arrived, I found I had no appetite and was proof against Mrs. Hudson's most earnest entreaties. While I drifted in the pleasing haze of savoury aromas, Mackenzie and Holmes managed to dispatch both their repasts and my own.

I had an indistinct recollection of being bundled to bed in my old room, my shoulder giving me sharp, erratic reminders of my injury in spite of Mrs. Hudson's appeals for care, and Mackenzie's and Holmes' efforts to be gentle.

The following morning was a sorry one for me. Years ago, I had sustained certain injuries in thc service of my country, and the lingering effects of these had, I was of the belief, inured me to physical discomfort. But perhaps it was my increase of years, perhaps it was the unwelcome memory of the sharp crack I had heard as my bone was fractured by my assailants of the previous evening; whatever the case, the pain in my shoulder had returned, sweeping through me towards the early hours and preventing me from turning, indeed from moving at all while I was abed. My face was swollen and, I guessed from my gentle prodding, very bruised. My lip was distended and crusted with newly dried blood. I struggled to bestir myself but could not lift my torso. Eventually I managed to swing my legs over the side of the bed and pivot myself up to a seated position. Tentatively I investigated under the borrowed pyjama jacket. Mackenzie's bandaging was slapdash rather than otherwise and I could see that the swelling had extended from my shoulder to my chest and under my armpit. Beneath the bandage, bruising was beginning to appear. I hesitantly tried to raise my arm and the result was a rather sickening grinding sensation. I lowered my arm carefully.

There was a gentle rap on the door and Holmes inclined his head into the room.

"Awake, old man?"

"Yes, just now," I replied. "Not too lively this morning, I'm afraid."

"No, I daresay not." He entered the room. "Look here, Watson, I need to know all you can tell me about your assailants of last evening. Mrs. Hudson has been the very devil at keeping you quiet this morning, and though I tried to stimulate your recollections last night while they were fresh, I'm afraid that your friend Mackenzie rather did for you."

"Ah, the morphine. Perhaps, Holmes, I have learnt a little sympathy for your own weaknesses." I began to smile but froze the movement when my lip threatened to open again. "I will do my best. Fire away."

Holmes seated himself at the end of the bed.

"You say there were three of them, and that they spoke to you?"

"Yes, one of them, whom I took to be their leader, said 'Now John Watson, these papers - let's have them.' I asked him what he meant and how he knew my name, but they closed in and began to shove me. I resisted, upon which two of the blackguards held my arms beyond my back and the other, the one who had spoken, thrust his hands into my coat pockets. I thought he was looking for my pocketbook of course, and I called him a thieving scoundrel. But when he pulled it out of my pocket, he checked inside it and just dropped it on the cobbles. He didn't touch the bank notes. Disappointed in his search, he leaned right into my face and snarled like a dog. Then he said something along the lines of, "Come now, Bert, let's us wing this bird', and that was when one of the other fellows released my right arm and swung at me with a truncheon."

I paused at the recollection of the sharp crack as my clavicle had fractured.

"And then?" asked Holmes.

"And then, well, then the other fellow let go and I fell to the ground. Not my finest hour, I am afraid." I sighed and shook my head. "They kicked me as I lay in the street."

"Your face?"

I nodded.

Holmes took a sharp breath and sprang up. “We have the performance; now we need to know the players. Come now, Watson, tell me all that you observed of these three men.”

“It was dark. There wasn’t much to be seen, just three men. About my height, I would hazard, and of the working class. Oh, one fellow smelt strongly of gin.”

“Indeed? And with half the male population of London’s alleys smelling strongly of gin in the evenings, I consider this narrows down our task considerably. Come, come, old friend, you will need to do a good deal better than that.”

It hurt my swollen lip to talk and my eye ached when I focussed on Holmes. I could not move my right arm without pain, and as I sat, I cradled my elbow with my left hand. Nevertheless, I racked my memories of last night with my best efforts. Yet I still had nothing to add.

“It happened very swiftly, Holmes.” I could not prevent a note of petulance in my voice.

Holmes stood thoughtfully in front of me, one long forefinger curled against his chin in pensive pose. “The fabric of their clothing? Rough, smooth, ornamented, worn? How did they move? Perhaps there is something you can say about their footwear, having such an intimate acquaintance with it. Now, you have recalled the gin: We have one smell, perhaps there may be others."

I was silent for a moment, then the thought that had tormented me all night exploded from me. "Curse those fiends! How in heaven's name am I to continue with my practice? I had just succeeded in coaxing some of the local matrons to bring their reluctant husbands to my surgery. Mary will despair. That poor angel of a girl has worked like a trooper to help me gain my list. Now look at me! Can you imagine the chatter? I shall be weeks becoming presentable again!"

At that moment there was a shout from downstairs, a harsh voice raised and the sharp cry of the Boots. Holmes was through the door in an instant, and I heard him taking the stairs precipitously. Without thought, I made to leap up, but staggered back onto the bed as though struck. To my shame, I lost consciousness.

Mrs. Hudson roused me some minutes later with a phial of *sal volatile* passed back and forth under my nose. Holmes was in the room, as was the Boots. I accepted Mrs. Hudson's steadying hand and once again swung my legs around to elevate myself to sitting.

"Now, now, Dr. Watson," she murmured gently. "Now, you must be easy, sir, you are damaged, you know."

I sighed painfully. "Indeed I am, Mrs. Hudson, I am grieved to admit. But what has happened to the lad?" I nodded in the direction of the seated Boots, in quiet conversation with Holmes, who crouched attentively at his side.

"Bless you, doctor, I am sure I don't know. First you last night, then this. Some rogues came to the street door not ten minutes since, and they treated him very roughly indeed. If Mr. Holmes hadn't come bounding down the stairs I could not have answered for the consequences. As it is, the boy's jacket is well-nigh ruined, and I am not sure his face will allow him to answer the door for a good while." She tutted under her breath, whether lamenting the harm the boy had sustained, or the cost of replacing a jacket, I could not tell.

I began to attend to the conversation. It seemed that in answering a knock at the street door, the Boots had admitted three men who immediately took hold of him and began cuffing his head. This was when he cried out, alerting Holmes. The men had the boy's arms behind his back, and one of them held some kind of cudgel.

"Did they speak?" asked Holmes.

"Yes, sir. One man put his face against mine and asked me where my master keeps his papers."

"And then?"

"And then you came, Mr. Holmes, sir, down the stairs at such a clip they let me go and took off."

Holmes slowly raised himself to standing, his hands thrust deep in his pockets and his brow a picture of deep thought. He glanced over at me.

"Well, well," he said. "Either a most remarkable coincidence has thus transformed our little domicile into an infirmary, or there is something in my possession that an unscrupulous party desires very much indeed. I incline to the latter view. I rather fancy we are under attack."

Mrs. Hudson clamped her hands at her sides and faced Holmes squarely. "Mr. Holmes, sir," she said with chin held high, "You and I may not always see eye to eye, and that's as may be, but this is my home, and I will stand up before anyone who threatens it and injures my household. You may count me as one of your force in this. Tell me what to do and I will do it."

There was a moment's silence as we three looked at this picture of determined strength, then Holmes snapped into action.

"That is all to the good, my dear Mrs. Hudson, for I rather fancy that the next phase of this skirmish requires a goat for our tiger, and, I trust you will forgive the analogy, you will make an excellent goat."

In spite of my infirmities, I chuckled as Mrs. Hudson's face transformed from the very picture of offence to an amused understanding. "I shall be a goat with the greatest of pleasure, Mr. Holmes." At that moment, observing the steely set of her eye, I rather feared for the tiger's chances.

Holmes was of the belief that the ruffians were watching the house and would make a move when they saw him depart, so it was arranged thus: Holmes was to leave the house with the Boots as evening fell. Mrs. Hudson was to sit in the back parlour, which opened from the kitchen off the area. I was to lie in wait, quite literally as it happened, as I was not yet up to a long period of standing. We would move a small sofa into the kitchen passage, and I would have my service revolver loaded and at hand.

With the kitchen well lit, the scoundrels would be attracted to the area door whence Mrs. Hudson, quietly mending by her parlour hearth, would be visible through the door on the other side of the room. With the adjacent passageway in deep shadow, I would remain out of sight.

We were prepared for a long wait. More than once I thought ironically that I was lucky to be in pain, else I might well have drifted off. Indeed, my nagging shoulder made comfort impossible as I kept my eyes fixed on the pane of glass in the top of the area door. I could hear Mrs. Hudson move about her parlour from time to time, and I thought it likely that the hours were weighing as heavily on her hands as they were on mine.

At length, some time after midnight, my eye caught a movement through the glass. I quietly raised my revolver with my good arm. Though right-handed by nature, my military training had habituated me to an almost equal use of my left hand in combat, and I was gratified now to see that my weapon was as steady as I could wish. My ear detected a stealthy scratching and the urge was strong to call out a warning to Mrs. Hudson. Suppose she had fallen asleep? Suppose these villains rushed through the kitchen into her parlour before I could fire? Aiming from the passageway through the doorway was like facing a proscenium: suppose I had only one shot as the actors crossed it, and that shot missed?

In the event, my apprehensions were not realised. The scratching sound suddenly escalated into a crack and the area door swung open. For what seemed a long moment, three heavily wrapped figures stood illuminated in a dramatic diorama, one with upraised truncheon: and then I fired.

Lestrade and his men seemed to flood the kitchen in an instant. They manacled the intruders somewhat roughly, even the man with the gunshot wound to his shoulder, I noted with grim satisfaction. I struggled up to go in to Mrs. Hudson, who was sitting in her easy chair, her mending on the floor beside her, eyes bright and flushed face all animation.

"Well, Dr. Watson," she said with some energy, "I find the life of a goat most stimulating."

Earlier in the evening, after Holmes and the Boots had appraised Lestrade, our colleague from Scotland Yard, of the circumstances, they had parted; the Boots to remain hard by Baker Street to watch the watchers, as it were, and Holmes to pursue what he referred to as a little exploratory venture, testing a deduction. It was not until close to three in the morning that the last of the official force had finally departed, their remonstrating captives long since taken away in a police van. The Boots and Mrs. Hudson had set the kitchen to rights, while, unable to help,

I had shamefacedly rested on the sofa, which two of the constables had brought into the kitchen. My shoulder was giving me the very devil, and fatigue seemed to increase the throbbing in my still-swollen face. My two companions, on the other hand, continued to effervesce with the rather unseemly thrills of the night's work.

"Did you see him drop?" exclaimed the Boots for perhaps the twentieth time, as he brought two of the kitchen chairs up to the end of the table nearest me.

"I certainly did!" replied Mrs. Hudson. "Just like a stunned bullock: a big, wicked stunned bullock." She filled the teapot and set the steaming kettle back on the hob, looking at me with some delight. "Dr. Watson is as fine a shot as I have seen, and I have seen some shooting in my time, Mr. Hudson being a rifleman in the militia. But there, look at you! You are exhausted, Dr. Watson. Take this cup of tea, and Boots here will help you up to bed."

The Boots took several slices of buttered bread into one hand, folding them first by their corners into his capacious mouth, and my arm in the other, gently helped me to rise. We made our way through to the stairs and up to my old room, and I was asleep before I had finished my cup.

The following morning, I heard Holmes astir early and I was ready for him when he knocked and entered peremptorily, rubbing his hands together with satisfaction.

"We progress, Watson; we progress."

"Indeed?" I was seated on the edge of the bed, preparatory to standing. "Were you abroad all night?"

"I was, and tracking a formidable prey, I am now convinced."

"Do I take it that you believe our three friends of last night were merely the henchmen of some other figure?"

"They are the chorus to our real protagonist – yes."

"I say, Holmes, it is dashed odd that you should use those words. I had a kind of sense last night that the whole event was a performance of some sort. Not that I have any doubt about those thugs' intent." I ruefully cocked the elbow of my injured arm, and even this slight movement caused me to wince. "I have come to the view that their truncheon was filled with lead, by the way."

"It would not surprise me. Perhaps Lestrade will discover it to be so. In the meantime, I believe I have come some way towards discovering who the real actor may be."

"In that case I will suspend my efforts to stand while you enlighten me."

Holmes tucked his long chin in towards his chest and touched his hands together, adopting his lesson style.

“You recall the Cleveland Street scandal? Not ten years since?”

I thought for a moment. “Indeed I do. The Prince of Wales’ equerry left the country, I think. Lord Somerset, was it? And I believe, were not the papers sued for libel?”

“By the Earl of Euston. There were, and he won, though at a pretty cost to his reputation. He was quite disgraced.”

“What on earth has this to do with our present circumstance?”

“Possess your soul in patience, my dear Watson. There is a connection if you will allow me to explicate. The Cleveland Street scandal alarmed the populace with one of its most cherished dreads: that of the aristocratic vice that corrupts working class lads. As a consequence, the public took unbridled delight in the sordid details that the press was only too happy to provide, you will recollect, at a penny a paper. Thus, we were witness to the most edifying of spectacles: the exposure of a rather select group of gentlemen whose consequent falls from grace provided the most salient of lessons for others of their persuasion. And what do you suppose was the result?”

“Perhaps these debased individuals had the decency to consider their hearth and home, and to stay their unnatural impulses.”

Holmes drew an amused sigh. "Watson, you never fail me. I am of half a mind to think you are teasing, yet, you do appear to be all seriousness. In any event the result was of course that these gentlemen bethought themselves to make discretion an even higher art that it had been heretofore. In other words, they did not stop at hearth and home, I am sorry to relate to an Englishman of your sensibilities, but went to ground."

"You mean to say that such establishments continue to exist? Here in London?"

"Here in London, my dear Watson, and I would hazard in Paris, in Hamburg, in Capetown, I have no doubt even in Sydney. And the clientele values privacy and discretion above all else. These are powerful men who do not wish to lose their considerable standing. Some of them would stop at nothing to prevent an exposure. Do you begin to see where I lead, Watson?"

No doubt a dawning understanding was evident upon my countenance, for Holmes, watching me, smiled and nodded sagaciously. "I see that you do. Our quarry, the lead actor in this drama, or perhaps the tiger to Mrs. Hudson's goat, whatever amusing analogy we choose to employ, is a gentleman of reputation and power: a gentleman whose appetites are overriding but are, unfortunately for him, not condoned by society."

"I take it you mean that this gentleman is determined to secure some evidence that would tell against him, were it made public? Hence his confederates asking the lad and me about papers?"

“That is precisely what I mean, Watson. This gentleman, if it is not stretching the word’s etymology too far to employ it, is of the belief that I, or a member of my household, is in possession of some incriminating papers. Since I am certain I do not hold any such evidence, there are only two possibilities: either I hold something in ignorance; or our adversary is mistaken. If the former, then someone must have secreted something here in recent times without my knowledge. I made a rudimentary search of the house yesterday – you saw me rummaging, I believe – but found nothing, nor could I recollect any moment when this might have been achieved without someone in my trusted circle, which you will allow is very small, comprising just Mrs. Hudson and her household of two, the Boots and the cook, becoming aware of the intrusion.”

I felt a momentary twinge at not being included in Holmes’ trusted circle, as he phrased it.

Of course, nothing escaped Holmes. He paused for a moment, catching my eye. “I need hardly mention, my dear Watson, that of course of all individuals you hold the position of most trust in my entire acquaintance. In this instance, I am merely referring to those who reside with me, which perhaps unhappily for me, you no longer do.”

“Of course, of course,” I said. “Say no more.” I cleared my throat.

“Thus, I arrived at the necessary conclusion that our adversary’s belief that I held such papers was erroneous. The most obvious cause for his belief must be contact with someone from outside the household, and as my work regularly attracts strangers to our door, a client or prospective client must be the link in this deductive chain. I had received just five individuals who had hopes they might engage my services in the past two months – rather a slow time, as it happens – so I spent yesterday afternoon examining the details of each case, which I had of course indexed. I knew that I sought a male client of some influence, which narrowed my search considerably. In fact, it narrowed my search to nothing."

"Nothing, Holmes?"

"In the time named, I had not been approached by a single person who fitted the criteria of a gentleman of influence. I confess I was at fault here, assuming that the applicant would be the individual himself. However, once the light dawned, shamefully slow as it had been, that the incriminating papers might have been in the possession of a third party, I went back to my records."

"And?"

"And I found Mr. and Mrs. Robbie Briscomb."

"Concerning whom you are no doubt about to enlighten me."

"I believe there is no necessity, Watson, as I expect them any moment."

In the event I had some ten minutes to painfully stand and dress and drink the cup of coffee brought to me by a still-animated Mrs.

Hudson. I was seated in the drawing room with Holmes when Mrs. Hudson herself showed the Briscombs in. I had no doubt the Boots was below stairs still wearing his bruises as a badge of honour.

The Briscombs were a well-presented couple in their forties, unmistakably of the middle classes. As Holmes introduced us, I could see their wonder at my condition. I apologised for not standing while Holmes explained that I had sustained some injuries in the course of our work together, and their wonder increased.

It was immediately clear that Mrs. Briscomb was a competent, organising woman and her husband the philosopher of the pair. Once seated, he placed a small Gladstone bag at his feet and began to hold forth.

"As I see it, Mr. Holmes, this has something to do with my wife's sister, Audrey Durkin. It was Audrey's circumstance that brought us to you some weeks back, you'll recall."

"Perhaps you will refresh my memory, and of course the good Dr. Watson knows nothing of this as yet."

"Certainly I will. Well, like most interesting stories, this one has politics at its heart." He gave a meaningful look around our circle, ending with his wife, who nodded briskly to him in an encouragement to proceed. "Audrey found herself mixed up some time back with an earl's son, a young fellow with no real prospect of succeeding to the title as he had two older brothers living. But then everything changed. One of the gents, the eldest, took a bad fall playing polo, and was despaired of for some months before he finally died of brain fever. Then the next son drowned mysteriously – there was some talk that he made away with himself, but it was never proven. Anyhow lo and behold the young scamp of Audrey's acquaintance was suddenly a fellow of consequence, as the title carried with it substantial property and fortune, both here and in the East, I believe. Despite these tragedies, his father, the old earl, remained in good health for a time, but when he took a turn for the worse recently, it is our belief that the young man realised there were some dark secrets in his past that would hurt his prospective standing should they come to light. No longer the younger son, do you see? These younger sons of the gentry seem to get away with murder and dishonour. It's a blight on our society, sirs, a blight."

At this, Mrs. Briscomb leaned across and tapped her husband's knee. "Robbie?" she said mildly. "Mr. Holmes and Dr. Watson would like to know what happened."

"Ah, indeed they would, thank you my dear." In his turn, he leaned across and patted her knee.

"Now, dark secrets. What mischief does a young man with deep pockets get up to? You might jump to conclusions about his friendship with Audrey." Here he paused and exchanged a glance with his wife, who gave an almost imperceptible nod. "I see that my wife trusts you gents. Well now, it is not what you might think. Audrey is not that kind of young woman. She is a different kind of young woman altogether. She has a circle of acquaintance that is very particular." He hesitated, clearly unsure of how to proceed.

"Mr. Holmes, Dr. Watson," said Mrs. Briscomb. "My husband, though a great talker in general, being something of an orator, is rather a coy man when it comes to the relations between men and women. And between men and men, and women and women, if perhaps I make myself adequately plain. Audrey moved in a circle of young people who felt that society would not accept them as their true selves. The higher the position held in society, the more severe the possible consequences of discovery. Audrey's position, like ours, was not a lofty one, but that of her acquaintance, this young man, had become so."

Mr. Briscomb shuffled uncomfortably. "Lofty!" he exclaimed. "By right of birth, not of achievement or honour. I tell you, these privileges come at the expense of ordinary folk, and where do we find the protection of our own authorities? This country is no respecter of the privilege it is to govern ordinary people, and with a constitution structured with laxity that it is, is there any wonder that the monarchical system resting upon it is in decline?"

"Now look here," I broke in, "I won't have that. Any fellow talking down our queen and all she stands for is in a fair way to a thrashing, winged as I am. There is no weakness in our sovereign, sir, nor in that structure through which she reigns."

"No doubt your sentiment does you honour, Dr. Watson, yet you delude yourself. You delude yourself." While I struggled to hold my tongue, Briscomb dabbed his upper lip with his pocket handkerchief and turned to nod gravely to his wife, who to my eye evinced some frustration in a slight restlessness, as, increasingly, did I. "One only needs to observe this talk of a depression of which the papers are full just now. I make no judgment, I merely observe: the working man has the vote. The working man will have his say."

Here Mrs. Briscomb interjected. "Yes, Robbie dear, all true of course, but not what we are here for."

She turned apologetically to Holmes and me. "Robbie speaks at Hyde Park on a Sunday. Sometimes his eloquence, well, you know, just as one can have trouble putting aside a favourite garment when it is wrong for the weather." She turned quite fondly to him, and, his diatribe silenced, he patted her knee.

"Quite right, my dear, quite right. Ran away again." He looked at us unabashed. "Now gentlemen, let's solve this mystery, shall we?"

He lifted his Gladstone bag onto his lap and produced from within it a rectangular tin box. "I believe this article will be familiar to you, Mr. Holmes?" he said.

"Certainly. I don't doubt that it is the very box you begged me to retain when you consulted me some weeks since."

"Indeed, it is the identical box, which in fact, you refused."

"Refused? Say, declined, rather. You must understand that it is impossible for me to accept cases where the client is patently withholding data."

"Data? There was no data, sir, there were reputations hanging in the very balance and discretion was my maxim."

"How interesting, Mr. Briscomb, when you consider that this is the very same view held by those individuals you wish to hold to account on society's behalf."

Briscomb blinked rapidly at Holmes, and I sensed his mind turning over the notion that he might be offering protection to the very privileges he professed to abhor. Mrs. Briscomb leaned forward and put a firmer hand on his knee.

"Robbie. Robbie."

He turned to face her and I observed her expression: enigmatic to me but of clear portent to him, apparently, for he instantly stopped blinking, looked down at the box and placed his hands firmly on either side of it.

"Mr. Holmes, you are right. I withheld information from you when we first met but I do not wish to do so now. My wife has somewhat clearer vision than I. I am apt to carry myself away with an idea. My idea now shall be to solve this mystery and put to an end the persecution being suffered by you and your associates."

"We have not tried to open this, Mr. Holmes," said Mrs. Briscomb. "My sister entrusted it to me in good faith, for safekeeping, and though she did not extract any promise in this regard, it was evident to me that whatever is in this box is of a very sensitive nature. Now that Audrey has disappeared …"

It was as though a bolt of lightning had shot into the drawing room and struck Holmes, scattering electrical currents throughout the room, instantly charging it. I could see the suppressed emotion in his outwardly calm form.

"Disappeared?" he asked quietly.

"Why yes, I thought you understood this when you called on us so very late last night." The couple exchanged a puzzled glance.

"Curse me for a fool!" growled Holmes. "I truly believe I am losing my powers. Watson! Get your coat." He turned to me and immediately recollected my damaged condition. "Never mind. One of you, quick! Time is of the essence."

Mrs. Briscomb started up at once and buttoned her jacket. "Of course," she said. "I am ready."

Briscomb cast a bewildered gaze at her, then at me. "Stay here!" said Holmes, pointing commandingly at him, upon which Holmes and the woman hastened through the door. A moment later, Holmes returned and, swooping towards the tin box, prised it from Briscomb's hands and thrust it into mine, before disappearing back through the door.

"Where are they going?" Briscomb asked me faintly.

"I have absolutely no idea. I shall call for some tea for you, Mr. Briscomb, but you must excuse me if I retire. I am not fit company in my present state. I dare say your wife is safe enough." I stood awkwardly, carrying the tin box. "Good day."

The truth was, of course, that I could no more remain in the room with such an unreflecting socialist, without the ameliorating presence of Holmes, than fly.

For most of that afternoon I slept. Initially I wrestled with the discomfort of lying down, exhausted in mind and body but unable to sleep for pain, until eventually I surrendered, and sent for Mackenzie, who, smiling wryly, administered another relieving dose of morphine. I did not stir until evening.

It was Holmes who woke me. "You will be pleased to hear that we advance, Watson, we advance."

I did not seek to rise. "You have found the young woman?"

"Not as yet, but my able assistant and I believe we have discovered her location. All the evidence points to her being hidden, not necessarily against her will, at an establishment of the kind we spoke of last evening."

I did not at first register the barb about his assistant in my astonishment. "But Holmes, this is dreadful! We must alert the official force without delay. A place of such vice, right here in London, you say? It is iniquitous. It must be stamped out." I struggled to rise, still groggy and now with shooting pains in my shoulder.

Holmes' chuckling infuriated me. "Perhaps a battle for another day, old chap: a quarrel for others to pursue. Our purpose is clear. We must needs extricate this young woman without disturbing a hornets' nest, and Mrs. Briscomb and I have a stratagem ready. We beard the den tonight in disguise."

"But, Holmes, is it safe? You have said yourself that these are powerful people. What will Briscomb say?"

"I rather think that Briscomb will say whatever Mrs. Briscomb decides upon, and since I do not have my faithful Watson at my side, I adapt. In fact, considering the quest upon which we embark, it is perhaps fortunate that you are not of the party."

This was provoking. "What on earth do you mean, Holmes? I have many times proven myself useful in a tight spot. What can this woman do?"

"This woman, Watson, can assume a, shall we say, sapphic persona as a means of entry, which even I, who hold your achievements very high, think a trifle beyond your powers. And I mean to accompany her as her gentlemanly counterpart."

"Holmes, this really is outrageous. No one knows better than I how masterfully you adopt a disguise, but this?"

“This. One man in his time plays many parts, Watson. Bye the bye, I see that you escaped our friend Briscomb at the earliest opportunity this morning. Mrs. Hudson tells me he bailed her up when she brought him some tea and believed herself lucky to escape before nightfall. However, he left soon afterwards, perhaps seeking an audience elsewhere, perhaps to await the return of his wife. Mrs. Briscomb, I must say, is an admirable collaborator. It seems that her sex deters her from neither hazard nor imprudence. I expect her return any moment, in the guise of a tribade. Ah! That may be her knock now.”

A moment later, a bruised Boots, who had apparently exhausted the pleasures of remaining hidden in the kitchen, showed a transformed Mrs. Briscomb directly into my chamber at Holmes’ request and in spite of my objections. She was dressed as a young blade: silk kerchief knotted at her throat; tight, embroidered waistcoat over flowing shirtsleeves; and, most bizarre of all, a pair of trousers. She carried in her hand an opera hat.

“Splendid!” said Holmes, “You shall do very well.”

“Thank you, Mr. Holmes, but Dr. Watson, please accept my apology. I had no wish to invade your repose in his way. I did not realise I was being shown into your room.” She made to leave, but Holmes stopped her.

“Not at all, Mrs. Briscomb. We are all colleagues here, are we not, Watson?”

I had no choice but to agree, in spite of my discomfort at receiving visitors while abed. I wondered what Mary would say. Holmes settled the two of them into chairs and turned to Mrs. Briscomb.

"I take it you were able to satisfy your husband of the necessity of our adventure tonight?"

"He was not at first amenable, but when I pointed out the risks that Audrey surely faces, and the impossibility of extracting her in any other way, and when I reassured him as to my own safety, he was quite agreeable."

"Perhaps a man of such strong political views is not always so persuadable?"

"On the contrary, Mr. Holmes. I find that Robbie takes many of his views from me, though he may not believe that to be the case. I must say that the result is at times a somewhat curious amalgam. I scarcely recognise my original thoughts in his orations, for example, though I frequently detect the ingredients."

Holmes leaned forward, his elbows on his knees. "How so?"

"Well, let us say I listen to my husband read the speech he has written for the following day. I might see a bold statement endorsing better political education of our young, a principle we have oftentimes discussed, but no thought of how such an enterprise might be managed. Or perhaps I see a call for general suffrage, another of my strongly held views, but detect a disdain for the political wisdom of the working classes. I am well aware that his anger at the injustice of hereditary privilege in this country is real, but so too is his deeply felt reluctance to mount any kind of challenge to it. Do I make myself plain?"

"Yes, madam, I understand you. You do not accuse your husband of hypocrisy; he holds certain beliefs but does not purport to hold the secret to making them realities."

"That is exactly correct, Mr. Holmes. He rails, and he does it well. I do not see my husband's destiny to be any greater than this, and I am content. I am sure you have observed that we are a happy couple. We neither expect from the other that which is not possible. The separation of the spheres, if you like."

Holmes gave a dry chuckle. "I hardly think our political philosophers were seeking the recipe for a happy marriage in developing the concept. It is a concept, by the way, with which I cannot truly agree. My increasing observation is that women are as adept at operating in the political and commercial worlds as men but are held back for reasons other than their own abilities. Why, just ask Watson. His wife is as politically engaged an animal as most of the superannuated fellows in the House of Lords. Is that not so, Watson?"

I coughed. "Mary does indeed have her views and her work." I shifted uncomfortably.

"Indeed?" said Mrs. Briscomb. "And what work is it that Mrs. Watson undertakes? She is involved in the suffragist movement, perhaps?"

"Certainly Mary supports the move towards universal suffrage, but she is not herself, that is, well, Mary is away at present, in fact, in Liverpool, helping some … let's see, a group of women are trying to establish a party, is it? Or a refuge perhaps."

There was a moment's silence as I registered both Mrs. Briscomb's disappointment in me and my own shame in the realisation of how poorly I had informed myself about Mary's exertions. I understood in an instant the grave disservice I had afforded her, and I resolved to make amends.

"Well," said Holmes briskly. "I believe it is time for me to prepare." Mercifully, he showed Mrs. Briscomb out to await him in the drawing room, leaving me to struggle from bed and dress myself as best I might.

I had just entered the drawing room when Holmes appeared in his role for the evening's enterprise. He was dressed as a dandy, with ruffled fronted shirt and deep purple morning jacket. When I detected a trace of powder on his face, I winced and turned away.

Holmes chuckled. "A little effete for our Watson, but admirably suited to our purposes. Come Mrs. Briscomb. Let's to battle."

"Good luck to you," I said as they quitted the room. I heard them descend the stairs and Holmes' voice in mock heroic tones: "Cry havoc and let slip the dogs of war."

After my torpor of the afternoon, sleep was not to be thought of through the evening, however inexorably the clock crept onwards. My shoulder pained me still, though happily the swelling in my face was beginning to lessen. I picked up and put down the morning's papers in a desultory fashion. I lit my pipe but let it go out. I opened Lippincott's journal, but even the latest provocative chapter from Wilde failed to capture my attention. At length, I simply reclined on the settee and waited.

When I truly began to anticipate the return of Holmes and Mrs. Briscomb, I heard a knock at the street door and the sound of the Boots seeing someone, clearly not Holmes, up the stairs. The hour was late and I wondered who might be calling, and whether they perhaps brought news of my friend. My heart sank within me, however, when I recognised the voice of Briscomb, offering some comment to the Boots as they reached the landing. There was only one door to the drawing room, and they were approaching it from the other side: I was effectively trapped.

"Well, well, Dr. Watson, I am most gratified to find you here." He turned to the Boots who was showing him in. "Thank you my lad and take care of that face of yours." The Boots cocked his head quizzically in response and backed from the room.

"I flattered myself that my company would be welcome to you, sir, knowing as I did that you would be waiting too, and that we could wait together, as it were."

"Indeed," said I.

He settled into one of the armchairs by the hearth and felt about in his pockets. "May I smoke?" I gave a terse nod and he offered me a cigar, which I declined.

"This escapade," he began, "this Holmes of yours. I do hope he considers my wife's protection. As I understand it, they are venturing into something of a den in the hopes of extracting my wife's sister. But do we even know she wants to be extracted? That is my question for you, sir. Do we even know?"

I made no answer, well aware that he did not require one.

"These people I cannot answer for. I do not trust these gentlefolk who choose to live on the edge of society and not at its centre, which we are given to understand is their birthright simply by reason of their being so called gentlefolk. Such a luxury, by the by, to be 'gentle.' One is led towards the view that, somehow, working folk can't afford gentleness; all they can scrape together is a bit of roughness – then these so-called gentle folk find the rough folk to be invisible. See here, they will tell you that London in July is empty. Not a soul in town they say, if they are unfortunate enough to be left behind at the season's end. Not a soul, eh? Yet someone is still cleaning their boots and cooking their pastries and mucking out for their blessed carriage horses. Why, a good three quarters of Londoners are working class, sir, and the better part of what remains is that class of people to whom I belong. The middle class, sir, and not ashamed to be industrious. Yet there is apparently not a soul in London." He shook his head in an exaggerated performance of bewilderment.

Again, I did not reply. This time he glanced up at me, and, taking in my bruises and bandages, seemed to apprehend how far his conversation had drifted. "Look here, Dr. Watson, can I get you something? I shall ring for some tea."

"Not on my account," I said. I am afraid my manner was gruff. Chastened, Briscomb turned to the fire and smoked in silence. I reclined on the settee, frowning at the ceiling in a slowly increasing anxiety, awaiting the sound of the street door.

Eventually, it came. I heard a slam and a hasty bustle upstairs, Holmes' voice mingling with that of Mrs. Briscomb and another woman.

"That's Audrey!" exclaimed Briscomb. "Thank heavens, they are safe." He scrambled from the armchair and was standing ready to receive them as they entered.

Mrs. Briscomb was the first to enter. "Robbie! Here you are. How good it is to see you." She came straight to him and they embraced, somewhat to my embarrassment. At that moment Holmes entered with another woman. Her features were very like her sister's and her clothing similarly masculine; however, there was something ineffably different in her air.

To my discomfiture, she made straight for me. "You must be Dr. Watson. Mr. Holmes has told me all about you, and the sorry consequence you have suffered in this dreadful business. I am so very pleased to make your acquaintance, Dr. Watson." She took my good hand and shook it firmly. "I have the additional pleasure of knowing your wife, Dr. Watson, and I have a great respect for her work."

Before I could gather my wits to ask her what she meant, Holmes arranged us all about the fire, and moving to the tantalus by the window, poured five generous whiskies, topping them up from the gasogene. He handed around the glasses and settled himself by leaning against the mantel, his back to the fire, facing us as though we were an audience and he a performer. To my surprise, he raised his glass and said, "I give you, tidy memoranda."

I gaped at him, bewildered. His evident amusement at our expense was reflected obversely in the blank faces of Mrs. Briscomb, her sister and her husband. There was a pause, which in my battered state I felt heavily, but which Miss Durkin appeared to find stimulating, her face at once becoming alive with anticipation.

She raised her glass high. "Indeed," she exclaimed, "tidy memoranda! To be celebrated of all things."

I saw that Mrs. Briscomb now took the joke, whatever the blessed joke might mean, raising her glass with an amused smile, and that only Briscomb and I remained in ignorance.

"For heaven's sake, Holmes," I grumbled. "Tell us what you have to tell us. I have not the patience for this game. Indeed, I am heartily sick of the business."

Briscomb, now my ally, said nothing but blinked up at Holmes.

Holmes tossed his drink down and put the glass on the mantelpiece, the better to perform his denouement.

"What is the single most redeeming feature of the middle classes?" he asked, and I foresaw that a tediously didactic explanation was to follow. "Come, come, Briscomb," he coaxed. "I am sure *you* have an answer ready."

"Well, the middle classes are assuredly the moral leaders of society," said Briscomb uncertainly. Holmes slowly shook his head and Briscomb tried again. "We are enterprising. We, we … why, the middle classes are the backbone of our Empire, sir: hardworking and businesslike."

"Ah, better, better. And to be businesslike is to keep good records. And to keep good records is to have evidence of all commercial transactions, is it not? Mrs. Briscomb, might I trouble you to pass me the tin box? Very good. Miss Durkin, I believe you can reach that chisel? Excellent. Now if I were a betting man I would wager that we are about to reveal a series of receipts, neatly tabulated, which detail a sequence of commercial transactions between a gentleman of some status and an enterprising, businesslike member of the middle class."

In spite of my irritation, I was agog as Holmes gripped the box between his feet and wrenched the hasp away. He dropped the chisel and withdrew from the box a neat bundle of papers.

He scrutinised the first few flimsy pages keenly. "Carbon paper. Handwritten. Ah, I believe we have the creature," he said quietly. "Indeed, I believe we have both of them."

He tossed the bundle on to the lap of Miss Durkin who seized it and read aloud, "received from The Honourable Charles Bagnall, £3 for the services of Thomas Williams," she flipped to the next page "£3 for the services of Harry Amos, £4, £5, Arthur, Joshua, Benjamin … good heavens, there are dozens here! These go back months." She handed the bundle solemnly back to Holmes. "It is what I feared and suspected, of course, but somehow to see so many young lads' names, and all those pounds going into the pocket of that wicked man." She shuddered, and her sister gently enfolded her hand. Holmes returned the papers to the battered box and placed it carefully on the mantelpiece.

"And now the gentlemen are owed an explanation," said Holmes, turning to Briscomb and me.

He related the story thus: Miss Durkin had stolen the box some weeks previously from the proprietor of an establishment she had begun to frequent. While she sought merely genteel comradeship in this particular demimonde, her suspicions were aroused by the number of young men on the premises who were clearly not patrons. The proprietor himself, a Mr. Jeremy Chester, she considered evasive and smarmy, and one evening, when she found herself outside his private office and knowing him to be called away downstairs for a moment, she succumbed to an impulse and entered the sanctum, stealing away the first thing she could put her hand upon, the tin box which was one arrayed with many, in the hope that it would contain some sort of evidence of wrongdoing. She took the box to her sister, begging her to hide it. Once she had committed this theft, she must needs allay suspicion by continuing to visit the premises as regularly as she had previously done. She knew that the theft was discovered a day or two later by observing an agitated Chester closeted with her acquaintance Bagnall, the Earl's son, who emerged from their meeting in an evident white rage and made a noisy exit, dragging Chester with him.

The better part of valour being discretion, Miss Durkin now apprehended that her safety was in jeopardy. With the search being taken thence, she decided that the safest plan was to hide herself on the premises, and there she had remained for three days, moving between rooms, gaining the kitchen in the early hours, until tonight, when she had been discovered by Holmes and her sister.

Miss Durkin turned to Briscomb. "I sent no message to you and Sarah, Robbie, for fear of imperilling you. I regret causing you anxiety on my account. I beg you will forgive me now that all is safe."

"But how did you know Miss Durkin was there?" I interrupted crossly.

"By eliminating all that was impossible, my dear Watson. We knew she was not at her own home nor at the homes of anyone known to her sister, nor was she in possession of any great sum of money that would enable her to disappear on the continent, for example, and I understood her to be a person with no connection to the countryside. I established that she had not made a report to the official force nor had there been any deaths of young women fitting the description whose bodies were not claimed." At this, the women exchanged a glance and shivered. "I knew from Mrs. Briscomb that her sister was resourceful and bold, and I asked myself what such a person would do in this circumstance. I concluded that she would appreciate that the lion's den is the safest place to conceal oneself if the lion is prowling abroad. Ergo, we insinuated ourselves into the establishment in these disguises you find so distasteful," here I noted, with some embarrassment, Miss Durkin's surprise at my disapproval, "and were able to find and extract her with our good friend, Chester, being none the wiser."

Briscomb was thoughtful. "So these lads were imprisoned there? Is that what this is?"

"Not imprisoned," said Miss Durkin. "They were free to come and go, and they received payment from Chester according to how many gentlemen they had seen. A small payment, certainly, for Chester's object was to line his own pockets, not theirs. However I am not blind to the irony here: in breaking up this establishment to preserve these lads, the official force will be taking from them their only means of income."

I could not refrain from an outraged comment. "Better to starve than feed oneself in this way, surely!"

There was silence for a moment, and I feared Briscomb would deliver another harangue.

But it was Miss Durkin who spoke. “Perhaps not the view held by these lads’ mothers, Dr. Watson. Honest work can be hard to come by, and when the family is large …”

I saw it. Of course, I saw it. I had attended just such families and I had waved aside their shame at not being able to pay me in my anger at their sad circumstances, which I then forgot. But I was bruised and irritable and worried about my injuries and my work.

“I am sorry,” I said as I struggled to stand. “I am not myself. I believe my own injuries have drawn me inward towards introspection and ill temper.” I took a deep breath and looked at Holmes and Mrs. Briscomb. “I congratulate you on your inventive success.” I turned to Miss Durkin. “I rejoice in your safety and your courage.” To Briscomb I said “I honour your commitment to principle, sir, and if I may say so, your uxoriousness.” He gazed in surprise at his amused wife. “I believe I have some amends to make. And now, good evening, all. I go in quest of Mrs. Hudson for I have a letter to dictate.”

# The Case of Mary's Secret

## The Case of Mary's Secret

I was dragged from a deep sleep by a brief but sharp shake to my shoulder.

"John! John! Wake up!"

I began to stir, but not, as yet, to understand. "What time is it? What's amiss?" I raised myself on to my elbow and saw by the light of the candle she held that Mary was all but fully dressed.

"Mary! Are you ill?"

"No, not ill, John dear, but in pressing need of your help."

"A patient?" I swung out of bed and began to dress. "Mrs. Ketch, I dare say. I thought she was very near her time yesterday, and this is number five."

"It is a patient, John, but not Mrs. Ketch. Make haste if you please. I have sent Effie for a cab, and I am certain I can hear it at the street door. And you must bring your bag." As Mary helped me with my shoes, she glanced anxiously towards the hallway. I could hear the unmistakable sound of a night driver cursing his weary horse out on the street.

In a few moments more we were closing ourselves into the hansom while a sleepy Effie shut the street door after us. Mary called an address to the driver and begged him to make speed. I heard him mutter – it was a considerable distance and the night was a raw one. Mary settled back into the seat and pulled her coat collars around her throat as we clattered on.

"What is all this, Mary my dear? This is not a patient of mine, is it?"

She took my hand. "John, dear, you know you are the best of men."

Well used as I was to her good works making demands upon her time, as admiring as I was of her dedication to less fortunate families, and as refreshing as I had always found her independence, Mary's words now struck me with an uneasy feeling of portent.

The occasional streetlight flashed a chilled yellow into our gloom and Mary read the unease in my face only too plainly. "Now John, you must not worry," she said, gently stroking my hand in both of hers. "We are on our way to one of the families I have been helping, but tonight something unexpected has arisen, and I," she paused for a moment, bent thoughtfully over my hand. "We," she corrected herself. "We need your help, and John," she looked me steadily in the eye. "We need your silence."

I did not answer for a moment. The cab was rattling us towards a grim new suburb on London's outskirts, the horse's hooves striking the cobblestones sharply in the otherwise hushed streets.

"May I know whether the secret I will be keeping would be considered wrong, by some?"

Now it was Mary's turn to remain silent. She held my hand more firmly and turned it a little this way and that as she considered her answer.

"Yes, it would indeed. John, I must tell you that I am bringing you into a circumstance where your skills are needed but it is one which could bring discredit down upon you were it to be discovered. I know that you value your honour above all, but I am asking you to trust me."

At this I loosened my hand from hers and wrapped my arm around her shoulder. "Not above all, Mary. I trust you, let the future bring what it might."

Some twenty minutes later we stopped on a wide residential street outside a darkened house. I had a momentary impression of steep gables, an ornate turret and bay windows. Mary begged the driver to wait, and when he grumbled, I passed him a half sovereign and told him there would be another. At this, he tapped his forefinger to his brim resignedly, and Mary and I hurried in through elaborate gates, along a section of what seemed to be a circular carriageway and down the side of the deeply shadowed house.

"You have your bag, John? There is illness here."

"I have it."

Mary gave a single sharp rap on what I took to be the scullery door. It was opened almost immediately by a dark figure holding a candle out towards our faces.

"It's all right, Anya," said Mary. "I received your message. I have brought John."

"Thank God! Come, come."

The woman ushered us in and hastily shut the door on the darkness. "He is in here, through the kitchen. There is no fireplace but as you see I have kept the stove burning for a little warmth."

The woman led us through the scullery into a warm but unlit kitchen and to a small room near the hallway that led to the rest of the house. With the three of us jostling through the narrow doorway, my first sensation was that we had entered a pantry, so confined was the space. The woman placed the candle on the floor, and I saw that we were in a cell-like bedroom with a pallet upon which a small figure lay curled under a heap of blankets.

Mary dropped to her knees beside the figure.

"Shimon!" she said, gently placing her hands upon the blankets. "Shimon, I have brought my husband. He is a doctor."

I gestured to Mary to rise and step back and I took her place on the floor. I looked up at the woman. "You must tell me what is amiss." She hesitated, and I drew back the blankets to reveal my patient. There was a moment of silence in the tiny space as I beheld the large head and misshapen chest of the boy lying in an obvious fever. His eyes turned to me, his hair plastered to his pale skin, and he spoke weakly.

"It's just a little shakiness, doctor."

I looked up at the woman for explanation.

"It is not shakiness that troubles my son, Doctor Watson." Her dark eyes were angry. "It is fever, and now it is convulsions. I believe you can see the cause of his misery."

I could indeed. The boy had manifestly suffered from rickets in its severest form. As I examined him, I found his long bones were distorted and his back twisted.

"I can see you accuse me!" said the woman. "Yes, he was starved and locked away as an infant. As his mother the fault must lie with me, you are thinking. It is not so!"

At this, Mary reached towards the woman. "Hush, Anya. John thinks no such thing. No one accuses you. Come, let us go to the kitchen and make some tea."

The women left the room, leaving the single candle, and I did my best to reduce the suffering of the child, talking gently to him the while.

"My body shocks you?" he asked me.

"By no means, young man. I shall start by reducing your fever, and perhaps you can tell me: do you have pain?"

He turned his face to the wall. "My bones do not permit me rest. When I am well, I can walk a little. When I am not well, I …"

My heart, hardened on distant battlefields and toughened by time, was wrenched by the boy's simple words. I could not imagine how he came to be so afflicted. Here in the great metropolis a civilian doctor sees occasional cases, but there seemed no explanation for as severe and permanent a case as this in modern England. His accent and his mother's told me they were foreigners, but of an educated class. I pondered as I went about easing his discomfort.

To our relief, and in spite of the biting damp, our hansom was still waiting as we emerged some two hours later. I had left instructions and some medicines with the woman, Anya, who had accepted my assistance with apparent sullenness, and Mary had promised to return a day or two hence.

As we settled in the cab, I forestalled Mary's thanks with a question.

"Does my promise of secrecy extend to every soul?"

"Oh yes, John. Anya's safety depends upon it. I suppose you are thinking of telling Mr. Holmes. Indeed, you must not."

"I was not thinking of Holmes, my dear Mary, but of yourself. Are we at liberty to discuss this very serious circumstance?"

She took my hand and, for the first time all night, a smile suggested itself as she nodded.

On our journey home I learned from Mary that Anya Dashevsky was born into an educated merchant family in Kyiv. They had been swept up in the grim horror of the Russian pogroms following the assassination of Tsar Alexander II. Her parents and her young husband had been killed, and she herself, a terrified and dispossessed 19-year-old, was sent to Siberia. There she was delivered of her child in brutal conditions and there she and her son would remain for nearly ten years, malnourished, desperate and all but forgotten.

"How came they here?" I asked.

"They were allowed to settle in St. Petersburg on their release, but the laws there did not permit of many freedoms for her. She could barely arrange any education for Shimon, let along resume her own. So eventually Anya arranged an escape, and they came to England."

"She must be grateful in the extreme to have found herself such a safe haven".

Mary looked at me aghast. "Safe? John, Anya is in hiding! Why do you think I extracted a promise of secrecy from you? She and young Shimon are in danger. If they are discovered, they will be sent back to Russia, and in all likelihood, exiled again to Siberia. John, it would be their deaths. We must do everything, *everything* within our power to keep them safe."

I looked at my wife's animated face with surprise. The distant murmur of trouble in the Russian Empire had barely attracted my notice in recent years as I glanced through the daily newspapers over my morning toast, reading only matters of immediate interest to me, or at times the sensational stories that I thought might amuse Holmes. As we jolted slowly home in the early morning, I was troubled by my blithe ignorance as much as I was troubled by the risks Mary was evidently taking on behalf of others.

Several nights later I was once again woken by Mary as she hurriedly dressed by candlelight. Glancing at me, she saw that I was awake and hastened to me.

"John, dear, I have been called for. No, no, please do not disturb yourself. I have no need of your skills this time, and an escort is waiting for me. I shall be quite safe, but, John, I may be some time. It is very early now, nearly first light, but I must travel some distance. Please do not be alarmed if I have not returned by evening. No, I will not hear of your accompanying me. You have a heavy list today and your patients need you to be alert."

Before I was truly awake, Mary was gone and a moment later I heard the rattle of a cab moving off in the street below. I cursed myself for a poor sort of a husband to let my wife set off in this way, with no idea where she was headed nor with whom, until I reflected that any person who might thus charge me, truly did not know Mary.

My patient list was complete by early afternoon: the usual succession of mild fevers, skin irritations, and lassitude had made their way through my surgery with a little grumbling, tired courtesy, and the occasional moment of cheer. All day my mind had dwelt upon Mary and her mysterious summoning, and I felt myself to be at a loose end. My restlessness, borne of some anxiety for her safety masking the pricking of my conscience, led me inevitably to pick up my hat and coat. I looked in at the kitchen on my way out to tell Effie where I would be in case of messages and took myself to Baker Street.

As I pulled on the bell of 221B, a woman approached from the other direction and stopped in front of the street door, facing me.

"Dr. Watson!" she said in surprise.

"Mrs. Dashevsky. How do you do, and how does your son?"

Before she could answer, the door was opened wide by the Boots. He greeted me enthusiastically, Mrs. Dashevsky somewhat more soberly, enquiring her name, and led us upstairs, the two of us too surprised to speak.

Holmes stood as Mrs. Dashevsky was announced and entered the room. He cast me an inscrutable glance past her shoulder as he greeted her with his usual suavity. "Pray, make yourself comfortable, Mrs. Dashevsky. I am most interested to hear what brings you to me, and since you have been brought by my old friend Dr. Watson, I am quite certain you have an interesting tale to tell."

"You are mistaken, Mr. Holmes. I do not know this gentleman. We merely arrived at your door at the same moment. My tale, as you call it, is quite a private matter."

Holmes paused for a moment, with a quizzical look from Mrs. Dashevsky's earnest face to mine.

"Indeed?" he said. "I had thought otherwise. But take this chair, I beg you, and favour me with some details. Do not trouble yourself about Watson, here. He is a great respecter of private matters, and as silent as the grave." He seated himself by Mrs. Dashevsky and lifted his eyes mischievously to mine.

My own expression, I dare say, revealed something of my confusion. I was flattered by Holmes' kind words but my duplicity in pretending to him that Mrs. Dashevsky and I were strangers caused me some little discomfort. I took a seat further back upon the settee and kept my silence.

Mrs. Dashevsky began her brief tale: she and her son had been anonymously sponsored to escape to England from difficult circumstances in St. Petersburg. She now wished to find her benefactor to thank her, however her efforts had so far been unsuccessful. She had applied to the organising group through whom they had communicated, but which had not found itself in a position to assist her.

Holmes looked intently at Mrs. Dashevsky as she was speaking. When she had finished, to my surprise he spoke a few words in a language I did not recognise. Mrs. Dashevsky was patently even more surprised than I, though she recovered herself quickly, replying to Holmes in apparently the same tongue and at greater length.

Holmes laughed good-naturedly. "I'm afraid my Russian is rather too sparse and clumsy to permit me to converse. Forgive me – I am at a loss already."

Suspicious for a moment, Mrs. Dashevsky finally allowed herself a smile at Holmes' easy charm.

"But how did you guess that I speak Russian, Mr. Holmes?"

"My friend Watson here will tell you I do not guess, and in fact there was no need for guesswork, with the unmistakable fricative 'h' and lengthened 'i,' not to mention the classic 'ts' sound for a 'th.' And yet I'll wager that you are mistress of at least one other language." Holmes spoke a few words more, this time in a tongue I took for a moment to be German but which I soon realised was again unintelligible to me.

At this, Mrs. Dashevsky laughed aloud. "Now you are Jewish, Mr. Holmes? But have a care where you place your prepositions, I implore you!"

Again, Holmes laughed good-humouredly. "I am afraid a poor Britisher like me cannot compete with a continental European's facility with languages. But let me understand a little more about this patron of yours."

Mrs. Dashevsky produced a couple of letters from her clasped bag and handed them to Holmes.

"These are all I have, I regret to say. My sponsor and I did not maintain a regular correspondence." He accepted the letters thoughtfully.

"I believe it to be a woman's hand," she said, "educated, perhaps an older woman. But as you see, the letters contain no address. They were forwarded to me by the women through whom I corresponded to make arrangements for our journey to England. The paper is of good quality but more than that I cannot say.

There is something else. I am afraid, Mr. Holmes, that I have nothing with which I can pay you, and indeed I believe your interest lies in matters of the criminal world. I feel sure you will refuse me on these two counts, but I had heard your name from someone I trust," here she glanced towards me, "and I felt I must try you."

Holmes was looking intently at the letters. He murmured distractedly, "On the contrary. The fee is not the objective; it is the curiousness of the circumstances. As for crime, why, Watson here will tell you that he has more than once heard me remark how the strangest of occurrences are very often connected with circumstances where indeed, there is some doubt about whether any actual crime has been committed." He gestured with the letters. "May I keep these? Perhaps your little problem is not entirely without interest. I accept your commission; however, I make one stipulation."

"Stipulation, Mr. Holmes?"

"I have no wish to breach confidences unnecessarily. If it should transpire that your patron chooses *not* to be found, there I will let the matter rest."

Mrs. Dashevsky paused in thought for a few moments before giving a nod. "I see where your thoughts are tending, and I accept your terms."

He asked her a very few brief questions, made arrangements for communicating with her, and they stood. Holmes rang for the

Boots who moments later was ushering Mrs. Dashevsky out. We stood a little awkwardly until the sound of the street door closing told us she was quite gone.

"I say, Holmes," I began. "I am surprised to see you accept this case. As a rule, you consider missing person cases pedestrian in the extreme."

"Ah, that may be so as a rule, but only the most rigid of minds allows itself to be bound by rules. Facts, yes, but rules become arbitrary when unexpected facts are tested against them. The unexpected fact in this case is the deception being attempted by both you and Mrs. Dashevsky." He cast me an amused glance. "I see you have the decency to look abashed, Watson." Indeed, in my mortification I did not know where to look. "Yes," he mused. "This is quite the most interesting little problem since the encounter with our friend Xiuying and her missing python."

"Holmes, on my honour – "

He waved dismissively. "Not a word, Watson," he said. "I am quite satisfied that if you are keeping a secret from me, you have a very good reason for so doing. Let us not refer to the matter again, until, of course, I have discovered what the secret is, an eventuality you will agree is almost a certainty."

"Look here, Holmes, I may be obliged to withhold the matter from you, but I give you my word that to my knowledge it is not connected to the matter of this missing Englishwoman. I am afraid I cannot tell you this secret, but I can at least offer you whatever assistance you might require of me."

"Very good, Watson. I accept your offer with pleasure. Let us collect our hats. We have an old friend to see, but first I will have a quick word with the Boots."

I knew better than to pester Holmes with questions as we stepped out onto Baker Street. It was the work of a moment to secure a hansom, and Holmes directed the driver to Marble Arch. In less than ten minutes we found ourselves in the midst of the Sunday afternoon bustle in Hyde Park at Speaker's Corner.

"An old friend?" I began, as we jostled through the crowd. "And we are to meet him here?"

"I expect to find *her* here, though she is not expecting us. Keep a sharp eye out, Watson. We are looking for our somewhat socialist friend, Mr. Briscomb, for where Mr. Briscomb goes, Mrs. Briscomb is highly likely to be, and it is she who is our quarry today."

I felt I saw a familiar face here and there, but not upon a podium: rather, melting away into the throng. More than once, I touched Holmes' elbow to point someone out to him, but by the time I had his attention the face was gone, and half a dozen strangers had pushed their way into the intervening space. Holmes, with the advantage of his uncommon height, soon descried Mr. Briscomb, and in a moment, we found ourselves at the back of a small crowd gathered to listen to him from his position on a low platform.

“My friends,” he exclaimed in his fine baritone. “I tell you, the rise of this Empire has scarcely begun, as surely as the tide swells onto the shore. You may mark my words; this Empire’s rise has scarcely begun.” He nodded gravely to the listeners, some of whom were conversing, a couple eating apples from their pockets. “I make no judgment but observe: the working man has the vote and thus our world changes. Look you to the House of Lords. Is it the seat of power with which we have hitherto become accustomed? I suggest not, sirs, I suggest not. I believe we may now look to the House of Commons for that authority. Yet where *is* that authority when the very citizens need protection? This nation, mark you well, this seat of the most glorious of empires, is, and I regret my words as I speak them, for all its glory, no respecter of the grave honour it claims. It governs us, yes, but has no care for the universal understanding of that very responsibility. Why, an inky schoolboy,” and here, Briscomb gestured towards a young lad darting through the empty space in front of him, “an inky schoolboy could tell you more about the French Revolution and Madame la Guillotine than he could tell you about the grab bag of statutes, judgments, treaties and conventions that we for convenience, or perhaps it is obfuscation, refer to as the British constitution. Friends, there is no constitution! It is merely a drawerful of untabulated memoranda!”

Puzzled by Briscomb’s equivocal exhortation, I followed Holmes as he made his way to one side where Mrs. Briscomb stood, eyeing the crowd. Her face lightened with pleasure when she saw us, and she immediately came forward.

"Mr. Holmes, Dr. Watson! What a pleasure to see you here. I know better than to think you have come on purpose to hear Robbie speak, but I am delighted to see you, nonetheless. Come, let us withdraw out of Robbie's sight. He is unfortunately easily distracted."

She led us a short distance then turned to face us. "How can I help you gentlemen? I assume I am the person you wish to see?"

"Most admirable perspicacity as ever, Mrs. Briscomb. I will not waste words. We come to you because you are likely to possess some knowledge that we do not. We are seeking a group, politically motivated, in fact an organised element hostile to immigrants. I don't doubt there are many who might fit that bill, but I regret to say that we suspect foul play, and I can only suppose the numbers willing to act, rather than to merely orate, might be small."

With a fond smile, she glanced at her husband as he raised his fist and declaimed to the onlookers. "Indeed, you are right, Mr. Holmes," she said. "Most of those who find themselves here on their soapbox on a Sunday afternoon are satisfied to go home to a good dinner."

As she considered her answer to Holmes' question, I found myself quite twisted with anxiety at his words: foul play. This was not the first time I was well outpaced by Holmes' quick leaps of deduction, but at that moment I knew it to be the most agonising. It was not only Mrs. Dashevsky's unknown patron who was missing, it was Mary. I grasped Holmes by the elbow.

“Holmes!’ I said in lowered tones.

“Calm yourself, Watson. We shall find Mary – you have my word.”

At that moment, and before Mrs. Briscomb could furnish us with her answer, a grubby face thrust forward between Holmes and myself.

“Mr. ‘Olmes, sir. Telegram.” The young Irregular, for such he was, darted away, melting almost instantly into the crowd, and I realised that the glimpses of familiar faces were of course some of Holmes’ stealthy acolytes.

He glanced at the telegram and immediately handed it to me, his eyes on Mrs. Briscomb.

“There is one group that makes me very uneasy, Mr. Holmes,” she began. “They call themselves British Nationalists, but they do not represent a Britain I recognise. There are generally a few of them here – I have seen them further on towards Cumberland Gate. Their language is of violence and the temper of their proclamations carries that most dangerous of infections, fear.”

I glanced down at the telegram in my hand, for the first time wondering why I had received a missive in the middle of a crowded Hyde Park. It was directed to me. It must have been sent on by Effie to Baker Street and from thence carried by an Irregular, no doubt organised by the Boots after Holmes’ quiet word. I ripped it open, and I believe my heart halted as I read "Don't follow stop it is over thank God stop Mary".

Holmes clutched my arm as I swayed for a moment, and Mrs. Briscomb cried "Dr. Watson, you are ill!" Without a word I handed Holmes the telegram. He considered it for a moment before folding it carefully.

"This is not the dark mystery you so clearly suppose," he said gently. "Rest assured that things are well with Mary and, if I may so presume, your marriage is safe. Now, collect yourself, old fellow. I am in need of your help." So saying, he took his leave of Mrs. Briscomb and led me quickly through the throng.

I was dazed and unresisting. Mary, I thought. What dreadful crisis has come upon us?

Holmes glanced at my no doubt blanched countenance. "Come, come, Watson. You know better than to rely for meaning upon a telegram, where more information is elided than encompassed, and where the writer is often in haste, little thinking what effect their rushed words might have on the reader."

We dodged an exuberant family, trailing tea cloths and carrying a large basket. "You think so?" I asked.

"Decidedly. And when the writer's haste has caused them to misdirect their earlier message, thereby ensuring complete confusion ..."

"Earlier message?" I replied. "There was no earlier message."

"Precisely. I expect you will eventually receive it and there will be a simple error in the direction, and that the message itself will make all clear. In the meantime, I am aware of at least four points of interest in this telegram that convince me that Mrs. Watson's conjugal affections have not wavered." Holmes glanced at my ashen face without breaking stride. "I see my inferences require additional explication. First," he extended his index finger. "She has dated it from an address in Cambridge, and runaway wives tend not to name their location. Second," his middle finger, "she takes the trouble to write 'thank God,' indicating relief. If that relief were her removal from her husband, she would not be moved to write at all, and here we might find ourselves guilty of the logical fallacy of ***circulus in probando***. Third," his ring finger, "she uses the expression 'it is over' which to my mind suggests strongly that she believes you will know what she is talking about, which it appears you do not. And fourth," all fingers now extended, "is the telegram itself: obviously written with a sense of urgency which clearly indicates importance in the mind of the writer. She wanted to catch you before you set out on an unnecessary journey."

"Journey? What journey?"

Holmes ignored my question and, swinging his raised hand forward to gesture ahead, said, "Ah, and here we are. Our candidates, I believe, are that ill-conditioned wiry youth yonder, or that well-fed gentleman over to our right. I discount the energetic woman against the path there: Some of her listeners' placards advocate education for women, clearly not a cause in our interest today."

I had to be content with this unsatisfactory explanation of Mary's telegram, for at that moment the wiry youth over to our left uttered a harsh shout from his rough platform. "Do we stand for this?" His ragged crowd of a dozen or so men returned his shout with a "No!"

"Look at our East End!" he declaimed. "What has become of it? I'll tell you what has become of it: One hundred thousand Russian Jews is what has become of it. You heard me, lads. One hundred *thousand*. In *our* East End. And what are they doing for us? I'll tell you that too, my friends. They are taking our work from us, is what they are doing. They are taking our work, and the bread from our mouths and our children's mouths, is what they are doing for us. Do we stand for this? (No!) "You are right there! We stand *against* this. And why? Because we are British! (hoorah) British to the backbone and British for our Empire (hoorah). Did we ask our free-thinking, easy-going soft as butter politicians to make us the dumping ground for Europe's scum? (No!) No? And still they come to our shores. Well, I say, no more! Lock the gates! Turn 'em back!"

We watched in consternation as his listeners roared in response. Encouraged, the youth then gestured towards the group of women near the path.

"And right here before our very noses is the brazen thing itself. The evil that pulls us down, that cuts our imperial tendons and brings our great nation to her knees. Boys, do we stand for this?"

There was a sudden surge as the men turned towards the women at whom the youth was pointing. Holmes and I instantly strode forward to stand in their path and face them. At the periphery of my vision, I was aware of other figures emerging from beyond the group of men, moving forward and closing in, but my gaze remained locked on that of a scowling individual not a yard in front of me. Holmes stood at my shoulder.

"Come, come, gentlemen," he said composedly. "I hardly think that this is the way to resolve differences of opinion. Good heavens, is that a nightstick? I rather think our friends in uniform might like a quiet discussion with you about that. Ah, Constable Aitken. You got my message then?"

Two constables had appeared at Holmes' side and greeted him quietly. The dozen men hesitated uncertainly, glancing back at the youth, who had not yet collected himself, then at the policemen. The tension diminished perceptibly, and the scowling individual in front of me muttered an oath and turned away with his fellow agitators. The youth, with a false air of insouciance, strolled away.

A calm voice behind us said, "We know these men. They do not frighten us, though they try. There have been some little unpleasantnesses in the past, but as you can see, we continue to speak out about the matters we believe to be important."

I turned and recognised the woman who had been speaking near the path. Her dark eyes were amused though her brow was grave. As I raised my hat to introduce Holmes and myself, I took in her modest appearance and pleasantly intelligent countenance.

“We owe you two gentlemen thanks for interceding in this way.” She gestured back towards the group of women, quietly conversing but with their attention held by our interlocutor. “My name is Eliana Volfson.” She extended her hand to each of us. “I am a member of the Women’s Jewish Alliance. Among other causes, we advocate for education for women, but I regret to say that we do provide something of an easy target for those whose grievances are more political in nature.”

Holmes looked thoughtful for a moment. “Women’s Jewish Alliance? I believe I have heard of you in connection with Lady Goldsmid.”

Miss Volfson’s face lit up with a smile. “Indeed, she is our patron and our powerhouse, if I may so put it. Louisa is now quite elderly, but still very active in our causes. Why, only yesterday she – oh, forgive me, Mr. Holmes, Dr. Watson. I am inclined to extol Louisa’s virtues rather too warmly. Well, I will wish you good day, gentlemen, and again I give you my sincere thanks.”

“If I could detain you a moment more, Miss Volfson,” said Holmes, “I rather fancy you might be able to assist us materially.”

"Certainly, I would be very happy to provide any help in my power."

"We are seeking someone - forgive me, it might indeed be more accurate to say we are seeking two persons, whose disappearances I believe to be connected, though one of these persons has chosen not to be found and the other has only accidentally made herself undiscoverable." At these words, Holmes cast me a benevolent glance.

Miss Volfson's face revealed her puzzlement. "But I feel sure that I would not know the people you seek. How might I help?"

In answer, Holmes reached into his inner pocket and withdrew the letters he had been given by Mrs. Dashevsky, handing them to Miss Volfson and watching her face intently as she unfolded them. Her eyes swiftly scanned the first letter and merely glanced at the second. Wordlessly, she raised her eyes to Holmes'.

"I see you know the hand," he said.

In some confusion, she folded the letters and held them towards Holmes, who did not at first take them.

"Miss Volfson, I have no wish to compel you to reveal a confidence, especially where that confidence protects another's safety. If you tell me that my surmise is correct, and that this person who signs themselves as 'your patroness' is in fact concealing her identity for reasons of personal protection, there I will let the matter rest and will inform my client that her patron requires no further thanks."

"That is the case, Mr. Holmes, though how you could know this …"

"Watson here will tell you that it is my job to know these things. Good day, Miss Volfson." He turned to go, but as I made to accompany him, Miss Volfson spoke again.

"Wait. You said you were searching for two people. Who is the other?"

"Ah, the other is the person I believe to be only accidentally missing." He replied airily. "I have every confidence that Mrs. Mary Watson will appear safely within a day or two." I felt my heart lurch to hear my wife's name pronounced by Holmes as though she were merely the subject of one of his cases.

Miss Volfson again registered surprise. "Mary Watson?"

"My wife!" I exclaimed. "Do you know something of this? Please tell me if you know where Mary is!"

"Mr. Holmes, Dr. Watson, I can see an explanation is due to you. Perhaps you would like to accompany me back to our office. I shall inform the others I am leaving."

Miss Volfson had settled us at a plain deal table in the corner of a small warehouse. We had refused her offer of tea and I could see by Holmes' tense expression that my keen anticipation of her explanation was matched by his own.

"You must forgive the elaborate means we employ to keep this place secret," she began. Indeed, from Hyde Park we had taken a cab, doubled back partway on foot, entered narrow half-forgotten lanes and threaded through the middle of a dimly lit, empty sweatshop.

"I suppose that the danger you fear is connected with the mystery we seek to solve," said Holmes encouragingly.

"Yes, Mr. Holmes. There are groups who would harm us, not because of what we say but because of who wc arc. Wc have come to England to escape the horrors visited upon our people by the Russian Empire. In my case, I came as a child with my parents. In many another case, their arrival is much more recent. We all share the desire to make known to the good people of England the terrors and the chaos of the pogroms. We believe that England has a duty to denounce the dreadful wickedness that continues to be perpetrated. You mentioned Louisa Goldsmid. She has spoken out for many years in this cause and with some success, but with that success came threats and danger, hence her extreme privacy and our own secrecy."

"Those letters were written by Lady Goldsmid," said Holmes evenly.

She lowered her eyes. “They were.”

“But Mary!” I exclaimed. “How came Mary to be involved in all this, and where is she?”

“Dr. Watson, it may surprise you to know that I am acquainted with your wife. She has been assisting us to care for some of the wretched families who find their way here in an extremity of need. Sometimes we hide these people for a time. Mary has helped us considerably.”

“And?”

“She is safe and well, I can assure you. Two days since, she accompanied Louisa, who is quite frail now, to Cambridge to petition the college to accept a newly arrived woman into the school of medicine. Unfortunately, Louisa took ill on their first night, but I am glad to say that the malady was short-lived, and we received word this morning that she had recovered, and that the two of them will return this evening.”

Holmes gave me a look of amused satisfaction.

Turning back to Miss Volfson he said, “One thing I do not understand. Why is it necessary to hide these arrivals? Surely there is no impediment to their settling here?”

Miss Volfson’s face was grim. “There is no *official* impediment to their settling here, Mr. Holmes. However, when the arrivals are Jewish, even if they are in extreme need, the poorhouse doors are closed to them. Their relief is in the hands of a charitable body of whom you may have heard, the Jewish Board of Guardians, which I regret to say has so far strayed from its mission over the years that it investigates every applicant as though they were a criminal, and refuses relief to anyone who has not resided in England for six months. If these were the only obstacles, they would not be insurmountable: We are organised and we have resources. But the Guardians take matters further: they actively repatriate any person they deem unworthy of the board's charity. Mr. Holmes, Jews living in Russia are not free. They are not permitted to travel outside the pale, so any who have found their way here have broken that country's law, and if forced to return, do so as lawbreakers and face the gravest of dangers."

We sat in silence. I recalled Mary's impassioned words to me, and my own blind ignorance of the dangers faced by Mrs. Dashevsky and Shimon, as they hid in the back rooms of an empty house, want and illness their close companions.

As though reading my thoughts, Miss Volfson went on, "We have been helping a woman and her son who have recently arrived from St. Petersburg, and who were jailed in the terrible prison camps of Siberia for many years. The conditions …" Miss Volfson stood abruptly and made her way to a large cabinet against a windowless wall. "In fact, I have her letter here." She retrieved a box from the cabinet and flicked through several bundles of papers. I turned to Holmes, but his expression was unreadable to me. Miss Volfson extracted an envelope, and unfolding the letter within, began to read.

"I had nothing to do with this terrible thing. I am a Russian Jew; why should I wish to kill the Tsar? Alexander II was far from perfect, but I had already learned to accept the little as a great deal better than the nothing. He allowed us – some of us – to live, to be educated, to pursue a life of culture. That may not sound like much to you in England, living as you do with so many freedoms, but I assure you that my family has a long memory and to be left in peace, allowed to have a home, was a great good. I had begun my studies – I was to become a doctor. But then came the dreadful night in Kyiv, and the false trial, a long march north, freezing and with child, to a prison many did not survive. My son grew up in a cattle barn. He barely saw a book until he was almost ten years old. His frame is twisted, his legs are weak. He believes that Nature has left him unfit for civilised society. I tell him, this was not nature! Whatever ills he has suffered are the result of the hand of man."

Miss Volfson was still for a moment, then refolded the letter and returned it to its bundle in the box, and the box to the cabinet. "This woman's child is now fourteen," she said, again taking her seat. "We have put the two of them somewhere safe. Louisa has many friends, who willingly turn a blind eye when they shut up their houses to travel abroad. But even so, if their hiding place should be discovered, these two would be sent back to their certain deaths. I am sure you can understand my passion, gentlemen." She put her hand to her cheek, as though to quiet herself. "Perhaps I have spoken too freely, but I feel certain I can trust you with these confidences."

We solemnly assured her that she could indeed trust us, and we thanked her and rose to take our leave.

"I had better show you the way out," she said wryly. "We don't want any more citizens to go missing."

Once through the labyrinth, we set off back to Baker Street on foot, hardly speaking.

At length, to break the silence, I said to Holmes, "You were right of course, about Mary being safe all along. I expect I shall find that first telegram at home waiting for me, and perhaps even Mary herself. I shall take myself there directly."

Holmes continued walking reflectively for a while. "Good old Watson," he said finally. "You have had what must have been a dreadful scare not so long since, yet you are generous enough to compliment me on that particular deduction. You do realise, do you not, that I have missed at least three vital indications for that one correct one. Until we spoke to Miss Volfson, which you will recall was an entirely accidental meeting for which I can take no credit, I believed we were seeking a different group entirely and expected a much more sinister conclusion, though perhaps my alert to the official force was not without its use." He sighed, and gently shook his head. "It is all an education, Watson."

I was surprised at his uncharacteristically introspective tone, until a few blocks further along he spoke again.

"I am thinking about our fellow men, Watson."

"Indeed?"

"Indeed. People will tell you that women are the emotional sex, yet once we allow that fear and anger and pride are emotions, and if we further reflect upon what we have seen today, we easily see that it is men who are at the mercy of their emotions. I don't say all of us, of course. For myself I can claim with some justification that emotions play little part in my behaviours. I am a logician, if I am anything, and I am certainly not a humanist, yet I can't shake the feeling that the work these women are doing rather puts my little problems into the shade."

I considered his words. I thought it likely that he was including me and my strong reaction to Mary's telegram in his analysis of masculine passions; however even if it were so, I found his remarks gratifying. I detected an unwonted humility akin to that which I was feeling. As a rule, I took pride in my calling as a physician, believing myself to be of value to my fellow creature who acknowledged me as such, yet here was my wife working secretly, for neither pay nor recognition, at the hazard of her own safety, to save and protect the sufferers. Indeed, it was true: Emotions, roiling in me, had taken their authority.

Shortly our paths diverged, and I took leave of my pensive companion to hurry home.

I permitted myself a dry chuckle as I stood inside the street door with the telegram in my hand. It was of course misdirected exactly as Holmes had predicted, with an almost illegible correction scrawled over the top of the original, hurried address. It was dated two days since. I opened it to read "Dearest John, gone to Cambridge to help elderly friend who is unwell stop can you meet us here with your bag stop love Mary."

At that moment I heard the street door open to the turn of a key, and Mary, flustered and a little windblown, came into my arms.

The following afternoon, Mary and I met Mrs. Dashevsky by arrangement at Baker Street. We settled in the drawing room where Mrs. Hudson had lain tea. I was pleased to hear that Shimon was a great deal better than he had been when I saw him a week ago, and was now up and about, regaining his strength.

"Mr. Holmes, Dr. Watson, Mary," began Mrs. Dashevsky with some solemnity, "I wished to see you today not only to thank you most sincerely for helping me. No," she anticipated our dismissive replies, "I will say what I must. In exchange for your willingness to exert yourselves on behalf of a stranger, I believe I owe you my candour: the truth about my dead husband." She turned to Mary, who was sitting in an armchair by the hearth. "I believe you at least can guess what I am about to say. I believe your good heart sees clearly into the hearts of others." Mary smiled sadly as Mrs. Dashevsky turned back to us.

"There was no husband. I was not widowed on that terrible night in Kyiv when my parents were killed. There had been no binding sacrament, no innocent pledges exchanged. No, there were harsh cries, there were blows, there was injury. I did not know these men and they did not know me, though in their contempt I believe they thought they did. Perhaps they were maddened by the tumult and the flames, the shouts, the cries for mercy. I was driven almost mad myself that night, but with terror. By morning, when I found myself shackled to a dozen strangers and thrown into the back of a cart, I learned to be grateful to have life and breath yet, for all around us in the slippery streets lay the bodies of our brethren, their eyes closed on this imperfect world for ever.

"And then, blameless as I was, I was sent away to prison. I wish I could describe it to you. Imagine an artic desert, and here is a bare, tumbledown stable. The cold is brutal. Everything is damp – everything – and the only heat is one poor stove in the passageway. Do you understand? Our gaolers knew better than to lock our doors. If we had not been able to crowd around the stove, we would have died in our cells. In winter there was ice underneath our palliasses. And here I gave birth, alone and terrified. Some of my fellow prisoners were grieved to see me so powerless to care for my young baby, over whom I had to watch constantly to protect from the rats, and they would share what little food they had with me, but the food was cold, dirty and often raw. We were all starving. Dr. Watson, you have seen what this early deprivation has done to my son.

"Little wonder then that I have harboured rage for so long it became my familiar, and I confess that my reasons for seeking my benefactress were a little more complex than merely to thank her: I wished to join her. Mr. Holmes, I believe this is no surprise to you. But now that I have been met with such kindness, the storms in my heart are abating. The time for anger is past, gentlemen. I have told Shimon the truth, bitter as it is, and our way has opened up before us with wonderful clarity. I will honour those who have trusted and supported us so materially," here she paused to look sincerely at each of us in turn, and to hold Mary's gaze, "by helping others as I have been helped. I will pursue my studies as I had always hoped and as my parents had always wished for me, studies that have been so long interrupted, and gain the skills I need. I have been promised assistance in Shimon's education, and now I dare to hope to see my son grow to be a fine young man."

Later that evening as Mary and I prepared for our night's rest, I sat her down on the bed and took both her hands in mine.

"You have humbled me, Mary. You know I rejoice in your independence, but independence does not of necessity require secrecy. Pray let us have no more secrets between us. You have shown great courage, but in keeping your work from me, you have denied me the pleasure of pride in you."

"Dearest John, my mind has been running with secrets, I confess, and the grave responsibility I was holding for others, but in believing that I should keep all this from you because you were burdened with your own cares, I have been mistaken."

I kissed her captive hands. She sighed.

"There is something I need to know, John. Tell me what sort of a life Shimon can hope for. Will he … will Shimon survive?"

"Yes," I replied gently. "There is no threat to his life. His bones will never straighten, of course, and he can expect to always walk with some awkwardness, but I think you will be surprised at the Shimon you see a few months hence, when he is well, and nourished and becoming accustomed to the safety of his new life."

"Thank you, John. That pleases me immeasurably." Mary rose to fetch the candle. "Now let us make an extravagant wish: that we will not be called for in the night."

"Ah, but you forget Mrs. Ketch. Her confinement is now past time. I predict a call at three o'clock in the morning."

Mary laughed. "Well, perhaps we can make an exception for Mrs. Ketch." She snuffed the candle, and peaceful darkness settled around us.

# The Case of the Secret Mission

## The Case of the Secret Mission

Not for the first time, I asked myself what it was that brought me back to this door. I stood outside 221B Baker Street, my hand poised at the familiar knocker, and took a breath, recalling moments of chaos, and of frustrations, and, if I am to be candid, mortification at the hands of my old friend Sherlock Holmes. And yet here I was.

Boots, the same boy as of old but now appearing to stretch out of his jacket with the extenuation of youth, answered my quick tap.

"Dr. Watson, sir! Why, it's a pleasure to see you sir! Come in, do." He opened the door wide and made way for me to enter. "Mrs. Hudson will be ever so pleased. She was just talking of you the other day, if you'll believe it, sir. 'I wonder how our Dr. Watson is getting along', says she, plain as day." He lowered his voice guardedly. "Her sister – you know that one at Hampstead? Was about to take that dog that time?" At this memory he paused for the briefest of moments. "Anyway, she is ever so poorly." After closing the door, he mounted the stairs and looked around for me to follow him up. "Not Mrs. H, you mind, the sister. But then again, a bit low is Mrs. H, I don't mind telling you, and it's not as though Mr. Holmes is cheery company."

At this, I cut into his surprising volubility. "Ah, yes, Mr. Holmes. How is he? What is he about these days?"

We had reached the top of the stairs, and rather than make answer, Boots shook his head and opening the drawing room door, swung it wide. "Dr. Watson," he announced, with an air somewhere between self-importance and bashfulness.

I entered the room with a little trepidation, not at all certain of what I might be about to step into. A three-ring circus, however, was certainly not one of the scenarios I anticipated.

With considerable astonishment I saw Mrs. Hudson standing in the centre of the room, holding her now fully grown fox terrier bitch out at arm's length with some difficulty. Holmes was standing unsteadily on the arm of the settee near the window, with a gathering of the curtains in one hand and what looked like a cowherd's stockwhip extended straight upwards in the other, like a ceremonial standard. The combined height of furniture, man and lash formed an apparition of startling aspect. The dog, which appeared to be partially dressed in a bonnet, wriggled with pleasure and let out a cheerful yap when it saw me. At this point Mrs. Hudson shrieked, dropped the dog, which seemed to bounce harmlessly, and came towards me with real warmth in her smile.

"Dr. Watson! How delightful to see you." She threw a stern look towards Holmes. "And especially right now, just at this moment." The dog cavorted around us emitting yelps of happiness while

Holmes dropped neatly down from his perch, letting go the curtains and placing the whip on the settee.

“Watson, my dear chap!” He came towards me holding out both his hands warmly, and grasped my shoulders. “Very good of you. In fact, you are precisely what this experiment requires just now. I shall put you to work *instanter.*” But Mrs. Hudson was not to be gainsaid.

“You’ll do no such thing, sir. Dr. Watson is to have tea, *with* my best conserves, and we will discover how his young family gets on.” She bustled pleasantly out, the dog looping in excited circles behind her.

My anxiety uncurled. I could not think why I had been so uneasy.

“My dear fellow, you have been sorely missed,” began Holmes, arranging us in the armchairs by the hearth. He reached automatically for the Persian slipper then paused, cocking an eye towards me. “This shag is perhaps a little rough, but…?”

“By all means,” I said, reaching into an inner pocket for my pipe. “Look here, it’s charming to be back. I can’t think why I leave it so long between visits. Though what the devil you were about just now,” I cast an inclusive glance around the room, “defeats me. But I suppose it’s all in the name of science, eh?”

“By no means,” replied Holmes, stuffing his pipe with the vile mixture. “There is no science in this. I am currently engaged on a mission.”

"You mean a case?"

"Not a case." He leaned in towards me with an unusual gleam in his grey eye. "A mission." He settled back into the armchair and lit his pipe.

I had finished filling mine and lit it, taking a few meditative puffs and with only the slightest cough. "My word. I need hardly say that you have never struck me as quite the 'mission' type, Holmes, old boy. Let me see. It's not a case … you had Mrs. Hudson posing in quite the oddest position in which I have yet to see her … you described it as an experiment. Look here, I'll tell you what. I shall try to deduce what it is you are attempting. I shall have, say, two clues and two days. What do you think?"

Holmes laughed heartily. "I think I shall take you on! What's that you have me so tediously saying in your cursed stories?" At this he waved his pipe around in a parody of sententiousness. "You know my methods. Apply them!"

I joined in his mirth just as Mrs. Hudson returned with a characteristically laden tray. Holmes muttered to me, "Behold, Watson, your first clue." I looked in puzzlement at the tea tray while Mrs. Hudson eyed us with affection.

"Now then, Dr. Watson, how does that angelic Mary of yours get on? And your little mite must be all of two."

We three did justice to Mrs Hudson's conserves and several cups of lapsang souchong as we sat by the fire talking about my domestic circumstances and recalling some of the more bizarre cases Holmes and I had been involved in over the years I had been his fellow lodger.

"But look here," I said at last, turning to Mrs. Hudson. "Young Boots said that your sister is ill. I am grieved to hear of it. I wonder whether there is not something I can do to help?"

Mrs. Hudson did not reply at once. She gazed into the fire, her eyes wistful, her mouth by turns trembling and determined. "Well, Dr. Watson," she said at last, "Ada is dying, and that's the truth of it. I know it, she knows it, but that feckless husband of hers won't see it, more's the pity. I'm trying," she said. "I go there when I can, and I try to talk to him. He won't listen to me. His type never will." She looked at me appealingly. "It's not to say he's a bad man, nor yet a bad husband. He's not." She corrected herself. "I *think* he is not a bad man. But he is weak, Dr. Watson. I believe I know what is amiss. He can't bear the idea of losing her, so he says it's not so. And he says it to the young ones, which he has no right to do. Making believe she will be up and about any day and taking them into her arms as of old, playing their wild games. But she won't, Dr. Watson. Any fool can see that just to look at the poor thing. Worn ragged, thin as a rake. But you know, it's not the dying that pains her, it's leaving those bairns, though her youngest has gone before not six months since." She turned her gaze back to the fire and we sat in silence for a while.

"What about her medical man?" I asked gently. "Is he sound?"

She made a wry face. “Sound? Chance would be a fine thing. Her medical man, as you put it, is one of George’s tavern companions as far as I can understand it.” I made to interrupt her with astonishment. “Oh no, Dr. Watson, I don’t mean as he is not a doctor of some kind. I mean he is a doctor as may have seen better days. A toper, I believe, and old fashioned in his notions.” She shook her head sadly. “I can’t help it but I do hate to see those dreadful leeches on such pale and injured skin.”

I grunted in disgust. The more forward thinking of my medical brethren had awakened to the ineffective torment to the sick and the weak of bloodletting. I fancied that this dying woman would be better served by nourishment than depletion.

“Holmes,” I said reflectively. “Are you busy just now? What say you to a trip to Hampstead?”

He almost leapt to his feet. “Just what I was about to suggest. I am at your service, Watson, old man.”

“Mrs. Hudson? Will you join us?”

“With pleasure sirs. Oh, with pleasure!” She hurried out to ready herself and I summoned the Boots to secure a cab to take us to the station.

In a little over an hour we were being seen into a modest passageway by a young girl I judged to be not more than six years of age. I knelt down to her, and gently asked her name. She shyly lowered her eyes and mumbled something I could not hear.

"That's young Emily," said Mrs. Hudson. "Say hello to the nice gentlemen, Emily."

Emily mumbled a quick hello then dashed away, leaving Mrs. Hudson to lead us through to the cluttered parlour. Baskets of washing were set about the floor and dirty plates rested on the mantelpiece and table. A cat erupted from beneath a chair and leapt away past our feet.

"You will please forgive the awful muddle, won't you?" asked Mrs. Hudson. "Only she's so ill." A stifled sob escaped her as she hurried from the room.

Holmes and I made space to sit, neither of us perturbed by the untidiness, or perhaps it would be more truthful to say squalor, that surrounded us. He had his own eccentric habits, and I my experiences in patients' houses to inure us. I could hear the children at play outside close by. A shriek of "No, Emily!" followed by a fierce "I will, then!" proved that the silent child in the passageway had a noisier alter ego.

"Are you ready for your second clue, Watson?" asked Holmes. It took me a moment to recall his meaning.

"Your mission," I said. "By all means, give me a second clue, though I have made neither head nor tail of the first. But no riddles – I can't abide riddles."

Holmes chuckled. "Very good, then. No riddles." He cleared his throat importantly. "My mission is begun."

"That's it?"

"That is your clue."

"I thought these clues would help me guess."

"Ah, but you are not guessing, Watson. You are deducing, remember? You are, if I may so put it, applying my methods."

"Your methods be blowed, Holmes," I said. "How do your methods help with 'is begun'? Why, my daughter's childhood is begun. The Boots bursting all his buttons is begun. November is begun."

"And yet applying the most rudimentary of reasoning would establish that none of these three could possibly be my mission."

"Look here, I do not even know what the first clue signified. You merely said 'behold'."

"And what was occurring when I begged you to behold?"

“Why, nothing. We were sitting in the drawing room, Mrs. Hudson was coming back with in the tea things, all very normal and regular. Nothing *to* behold.”

Holmes made a small grunt of amusement. “As ever, my friend, you see but you do not observe.”

At that moment, Mrs. Hudson returned. “No sign of George, and all the children just anyhow. I’ll hazard his shilling is crossing the counter at that wretched Slaughterer’s Arms.” She tched in disapproval. “But there, Ada will see you, Dr. Watson. She is …” Mrs. Hudson hesitated. “She is no better.” She turned sorrowfully away and led me to the woman’s bedroom, leaving Holmes alone amongst the clutter.

I found the patient lying restlessly in a dim room, bundled in mismatched bedding yet shivering with cold. A strong sickroom odour seemed to have seeped into the very furniture: I could detect bile, sweat and worse. Her eyes were startlingly prominent and her face grey and drawn. I did not need my stethoscope to hear her ragged breathing.

Mrs. Hudson leant down and spoke gently to her. “Here’s the doctor, Ada. Dr. Watson come to see you.”

At this the woman turned her pitiful face towards me and said, “You cannot help. Such pain, doctor, in every bone. I feel so dreadfully weary, I cannot tell you. And yet I toss all night, cannot sleep, cannot lie still. My husband cannot abide me, and the children –" Here she gasped, and tears coursed freely down her face. "My own little ones won't come to me."

"That's not so, Ada dear," interrupted Mrs. Hudson. "You know they think the world of you." She tugged at the eiderdown, attempting to straighten it, and I saw that her fussing vexed the irritated patient.

"I say, Mrs. Hudson," said I. "Perhaps you could bring us a cup of tea?" Mrs. Hudson paused and looked from her sister to me.

"Of course, Doctor," she said, and quitted the room.

I sat beside the bed, observing my patient intently. "Now then, Mrs. … ?"

"It's Gilbert. Ada Gilbert."

"Mrs. Gilbert. You've been taking some medicine until recently?"

"Oh no, Doctor. I haven't had any medicine. And I know well enough there's nothing can fix me, now."

"But you did have something that made you feel better once?"

She turned her head fitfully from side to side. "Well, yes, there was a tonic. George used to bring it to me. I felt the better for it for a little while, but that was before I got so bad. It wouldn't touch what ails me now. And anyway, there's precious little money for tonics and suchlike." She drew her thin arms out from under the bedclothes and I saw the marks of leeches, angry on the pale skin. She rubbed her face and shook her hands. "I swear," she said mournfully, "if the house was to burn down and all my kith with it, I doubt I'd stir to save myself."

I gently questioned her, and she answered in uncomfortable fits and starts, until Mrs. Hudson came in with tea and some buttered penny loaf.

We secured a carriage to ourselves in the homeward train. Holmes had been silent but attentive in a way I thought unusual, Mrs. Hudson anxious and fussy.

"Well, Doctor?" she asked, as we settled in, removing our outer layers. With a kind nod, Holmes took Mrs. Hudson's hat and placed it on the upper rack. He then gently hung her coat on the hook near the carriage door before arranging his own things. I placed my own on the seat beside me.

"Mrs. Hudson," I said, pausing to choose my words carefully. "Your sister has indeed the appearance of a grave illness, and I can easily conceive your anxiety regarding her and the fate of her children."

Mrs. Hudson said nothing but looked steadily into my eyes. I observed Holmes subtly tilt his head in an alert gesture of curiosity, and I saw that I had his attention to a rare degree.

I continued. "However, I believe your sister is not as ill as she appears. I believe this doctor who has been leeching her has entirely missed the simple cause of her condition, a condition, if I am indeed right, that we may attempt to reverse."

"What do you mean, Dr. Watson? For heaven's sake, do you mean there is hope?"

"Mrs. Hudson, it may take many months, but I believe I can return your sister to health." She was for a moment frozen and Holmes, for possibly the first time in my many years of knowing him, I had absolutely taken by surprise.

Then they both spoke at once. I steadied them with a gesture and commenced my explanation.

"When your sister lost her youngest child, I am sure she was not unnaturally overcome with a dreadful and devouring sorrow."

"That is so," said Mrs. Hudson sadly. "Such a common lot for women, yet not a one knows how to bear it."

"Well, I believe that somehow, perhaps it was at the hand of her husband George, she began to take a tonic which she felt did her some good. I would hazard that the tonic was a preparation of tincture of opium. Laudanum."

"Very likely. I know we tried what we could to rouse her in those months. I myself brought her many a preparation. But there's nothing amiss there, is there?"

"It is commonplace enough, I grant you, but for some patients it can become an evil worse than their malady. The body adjusts itself to the dose and then cannot do without it. And if the dose is stopped, the body rebels. Your sister's illness is – in my opinion, I hasten to say – her system's desperate need for laudanum. And make no mistake, the illness itself is very real."

"Indeed it is," said Mrs Hudson with some emotion. "I have nursed Ada when she is quite racked with retching, though she has precious little to bring. She can barely taste her food and as you saw, she is wasting. But, Dr. Watson, Ada has never said a thing about this."

"I believe she does not know. It is certainly an unusual situation, but she sincerely believes she is dying, and I saw myself how it grieves her to contemplate leaving her children motherless. There is no subterfuge here. She does not know."

Holmes had been gazing abstractedly out of the carriage window. He now turned to me. "A fascinating circumstance. How do you read the absent husband, Watson? Does Mr. George Gilbert know the cause of his wife's acute physical distress?"

"Ah, there you have me," I replied, shaking my head. "To be frank, I cannot make that out. Is he at the mercy of these overwhelming circumstances, or is he in some wise a villain?"

Holmes positively hummed with supressed vigour. "And there we divide our labours, Watson. You to the medical remedies, I to the conundrum of human action. Mrs. Hudson, we are at your service."

Holmes sent around a note to me the following afternoon just as I was finishing my surgery for the day. It read "Husband comes at 6. You?" I smiled to myself as I wrote my reply: "Naturally."

It wanted only a few minutes of the hour as I mounted the stairs to the drawing room behind the voluble Boots. I scarcely listened as he rattled off the changes he had noted in Mrs. Hudson since the previous day. "Don't know as what you've done, Doctor Watson, but she is ever so chirpy. Didn't scold me for a little whistling as I forgot not to do. And said nothing to Mr. Holmes' loud cracks, though I wish she would do so as they fair deafen me. Here's the doctor, sir," as he saw me into the drawing room and quickly shut the door on us.

Holmes was holding his whip of yesterday. "Ah. Now just watch this, Watson. It is an art, in spite of being colonial in origin." At this he held the woven leather shaft out in front of him with the four-foot tail hanging down from its end. He raised his long arm towards the ceiling and paused. I instinctively flinched as he brought the whip down smartly towards the floor and a deafening crack reverberated through the room. Holmes smiled complacently as I held my ringing ears.

"Confound your tricks!" I exclaimed. "What do you mean by this?"

He chuckled. “A new skill, Watson old man. I came across the whip in a case I was working on and fancied I would like to try.” At this he put the whip down on the table and removed a plug of cotton wadding from each ear.

“Devil take you. I cannot hear from your infernal toy.”

Not at all discomposed, he settled himself into an armchair and motioned me to the other. I complied with a sigh of resignation and waited for the ringing in my ears to subside.

“Now, this fellow Gilbert sent a telegram to our good Mrs. Hudson this morning asking her if he might call upon us.”

“Well, this is unexpected.”

“By no means. I precipitated this visit by myself sending a telegram last night to Gilbert.”

“You did? On what grounds?”

“I merely asked him to discuss with us his wife’s unusual circumstance in the hope he could throw a little light upon it.”

“Those words mean nothing, Holmes.”

“Indeed, and therein their value lies. Present a guilty man with a telegram that talks of throwing light upon a circumstance and he will at once leap to a defensive position, and you know of old that there is nothing more revealing than the defences of a guilty person."

"You believe him guilty then?"

Holmes tilted his head meditatively. "Guilty of something in this pitiful story, you may be sure. Guilty of what, remains to be seen. Ah, I believe I hear him at the street door."

The man shown in by Boots held a hat as shapeless as his suit was threadbare, but most conspicuous was his air of defeat. Holmes made his introductions and showed our visitor to the basket chair while we took the armchairs.

"You wished to see me, sir?"

"Indeed, we did, Mr. Gilbert. As you know, we have our connection with your wife's sister." Here he glanced around the room, indicating his status as Mrs. Hudson's lodger. "So naturally Dr. Watson here, and I myself, are most concerned about your wife's unhappy condition. I believe you know that Dr. Watson examined her yesterday."

Gilbert dipped his head, and gently flapped his hat against his ankle. Looking up, he began awkwardly,

"I'm sorry, gents, but I am afraid I am not able to pay you for your time if that's what you're asking. Things are considerable tight just now."

Holmes and I hastened to assure him that this was not in question, an assurance at which he was visibly relieved. “Then I don’t see how it is I can help, sirs, and I have left the young ones in the care of our neighbour, who, well …”

“We shan’t keep you a moment longer than is essential, Mr. Gilbert. Just one or two little points. Was it you who gave your wife the laudanum when your child died?”

He started and looked from Holmes’ face to mine. “Laudanum, sir?”

“Tincture of opium,” I said. “Perhaps in a tonic, perhaps as a medicine. Was it you?”

The room was still as he considered his answer. After a few moments he drooped even further, sinking into the basket chair with an air of profound surrender.

“You have me.” He sighed. “Yet I meant no harm, nor yet lies, to Ada, and never to the little ones. I know that Elsie, your Mrs. Hudson, that is, considers me confounded low. Fact is, I have been forced to ask loans of her, and nothing brings a man lower in his own mind than to beg of a woman. I have been brought down, gents, and no mistake.”

I found his self-absorption most distasteful. “Yes, yes,” I interrupted. “But we are speaking of your wife. The medicine.”

With some effort, he resumed. “Well, I knew a doctor, say apothecary rather, local. Someone I could ask.” I envisaged the tavern companion of Mrs. Hudson’s surmise. “And he began giving me a tonic for her. It cheered her considerable, and he kept giving it me. I asked him what it was, and he told me it was just the usual things. Then he began to charge me for it, which I paid up for a bit, then when my work slowed, and the young ones’ needs, and Ada not up and about, well, I couldn’t, could I?” He dipped his chin to his chest and drew in a deep breath. “But she was getting worse, and mortal low in spirits. She kept asking me for something, anything, so I gave her what I could. Tisanes really, mostly water, but in those same little bottles.” Here he looked up with pain. “To fool her, d’you see? To trick her. Because I wasn’t man enough to care for her properly.”

“Mr. Gilbert,” I said, “What was in these tisanes?”

“Oh, merely herbs. Wormwood, tansy, whatever was alive in our little bit of garden. I would make a tea and put it into the bottles.”

“And you also had her leeched?”

“Well, yes, my friend has many a time offered to see to her and charged me nothing for it. And very grateful I was, though truth to tell it did not seem to bring her up.”

“Mr. Gilbert, sir, your folly in both cases has compounded your wife’s condition.”

He looked, if anything, even more stricken. I explained to him the toxic qualities of these particular herbs when administered to a constitution as lowered as his wife's had become. I also dismissed out of hand the bloodletting as obsolete quackery.

"Mr. Gilbert, your wife needs nourishment and attention now. Do you understand me? No more leeches, no more tisanes, unless they be of comfrey, perhaps, or parsley. Sage is wholesome also. As for food, good plain soups with meat, and if you are needful there, we can ensure Mrs. Hudson's aid. Cool water to drink, clean bedclothes, soft flannels for washing. And above all, she needs her children about her. She needs her spirits lifted and sustained."

"But the illness?"

"The illness will pass, Mr. Gilbert. I believe you know what ails her. I believe you know she suffers grievously from her spell with laudanum, and yet you have deliberately kept her in ignorance of her real circumstance. If I had examined her sooner, I would have recommended a continued dose, but a gradually decreasing one. While she would have suffered considerable discomfort, she would not have taken to her bed, abandoned her children and – if I am to be frank with you, sir – lost all hope of this earthly life. In short, she would not have been so dangerously close to death. However, as she has already endured some painful weeks without the drug, the best course now is to persevere, but to persevere with hope, Mr. Gilbert, and with care. It is your duty."

I was barely able to suppress my anger at this fool's harmful actions. I turned to Holmes who had remained silent for some minutes. "Well, Holmes?" I said. "What say you?"

Holmes slowly drew his palms together and apart, together and apart. Abruptly he rose from his seat and paced the room. Facing the window, he looked down to the street below and said, "Do you recall, Watson, my remark in the train yesterday about how we would divide our labours?"

"Certainly I do: I was to address the medical; you the human."

"And you have acquitted yourself admirably. Now I take my turn." He pivoted on one heel to face the abject Gibson. "There is a little more to this story, is there not? Pray enlighten us."

"No sir. I don't take your meaning."

"This apothecary friend of yours. You say you were no longer able to pay him for the tonic, yet he subsequently attended and treated your wife without charge. There seems a discrepancy here."

"He, that is …"

"The apothecary?"

"*Yes*, the blasted apothecary. He did not attend my wife in person. It was his boy, his apprentice."

I groaned aloud in frustration at this careless usage of the woman.

Holmes pressed Gilbert. "You allowed an apprentice to let the blood of your gravely ill wife. Very good, proceed with your most interesting narrative."

"Damn your eyes! I had no choice, I tell you. I had to allow it or he – "

"Yes, Mr. Gilbert? Does this awkward position you found yourself in at all concern the missing laudanum?"

At this, the wretched man's imprecations fell silent. Holmes patiently closed his eyes and I watched them both.

Finally, Gilbert spoke. "What do you know, you fiend? Upon my soul, I meant no harm. I knew the youth from the Slaughterer's Arms, where I drank with his master, the apothecary. The youth had been stealing the tonic for me, for a few shillings. He could get no more each time or his master would have discovered the theft. I saw that it restored Ada a little, so one day I tried it, for I was in no good wise myself. The devil take that tonic! It made me feel better too. So I began to share it, but very soon I was taking all he could find for me and giving Ada the tisanes instead. That's when she came to believe she was really dying, for the way she saw it, she was taking the same tonic but the good had gone out of it, and that's when she truly became ill. I couldn't bear to tell her what had happened and what I had done to her, so I made out she wasn't ill. And I turned my back on her. I turned my back."

"How came that youth to be leeching your wife?" asked Holmes quietly.

"He had me; don't you see? He's an ambitious lad, that one. Once he had puzzled out what I was doing with Ada's tonic, why, he had me. He wanted practice, and I had to give it him."

I thought of Mrs. Gilbert's wasted frame, her corporeal condition a sorrowful manifestation of her spiritual misery, being made an experiment by a clumsy, ignorant youth from a tavern. Without thought, I rose from my chair. I believe my countenance spoke for me, for the craven Gilbert cowered.

"Don't hurt me, sirs! I suffer so. You cannot know how hard I am pressed. I beg of you, let me be."

Holmes spoke in disgust. "Let the wretch go, Watson." Then he suddenly lunged towards Gilbert, who leapt from his chair and banged out through the door. We heard him bounding down the stairs and the street door slammed.

"Yes," said Holmes, "unspeakable. Now, let us consult with the good Mrs. Hudson about how best to remedy her sister's unhappy circumstances."

He rang for the Boots, asking him to call Mrs. Hudson in. While we awaited her, I collected my thoughts.

"I say, Holmes, I am ready to try with my deduction."

His eyes were fixed far off, and I spoke again before he heard me. “Deduction?”

“Your mission,” said I. “I believe I have it. The first clue was Mrs. Hudson herself, and the second, that the mission was underway when we visited her ill sister. Now, what links Mrs. Hudson, her sister’s illness, and you? Not simply the medical crisis – you made that clear. It was about the human element. Yet, you did not know the sister. Ergo, you were concerned, I believe, about Mrs Hudson herself. Your ‘mission’, as you call it, was to aid Mrs. Hudson in her present distress. Your wild circus when I called yesterday was not an experiment at all – it was a diversion. Holmes, I believe I have found you out. I see you have a human heart, and that it stirred you to make yourself ridiculous in the aid of your dear friend. Admit it, I am right.”

Holmes gave a low chuckle. “You are right, Watson, as to fact but not as to motive.”

“Whatever do you mean, old fellow?”

“It is indeed the case that I have been attempting to divert Mrs. Hudson – to cheer her – and I was gratified when you chose to join the engagement, for a medical element was unquestionably wanting. But in inferring that I did so from motives of emotion, you err.”

“Nonsense, Holmes. You care for her; you know you do.”

"I care *about* her, indeed. She provides my shelter and sustenance. Did you not think through the pattern of occurrences that would have transpired should the good Mrs. Gilbert have in fact died? I should have been turned out, and I would rather not be turned out. I am most comfortable here."

"Turned out? How so?"

"Well, old chap, you know the odium in which Mrs. Hudson holds our friend Gilbert? And her fondness for her sister's children?"

"Indeed I do," I replied. "Our Mrs. Hudson is a principled woman and an affectionate sister."

"Do you see that principled woman and affectionate sister leaving those youngsters to be raised in disorder and bedlam by that object of revulsion? I think not: she would immediately bring them here. Now recall if you will, my good landlady's inexplicable aversion to explosions, firearms, chemical experiments and members of the criminal classes. If we introduce into the equation a need for her to put these small relatives of hers somewhere, why, I think we may take it as read that she would put them in my rooms. Ergo, Holmes is evicted, turned out, seeking shelter and sustenance elsewhere."

I gave him a long and speculative look. "So your mission was to help Mrs. Hudson in order to retain your lodgings, and nothing more?"

"Nothing more. If I could not cure her sister, I could at least endear myself to her."

"I don't believe you, Holmes."

At that moment Mrs. Hudson entered the room and we three set about our plan for the recovery of Ada Gilbert.

A little later and after a liberal tea, I rose to take my leave. Mrs. Hudson had gone to put up a package of provender for her sister's family. As I picked up my hat and made for the door, I turned to Holmes.

"What about this Gilbert?" said I. "He has behaved abominably, yet I suppose there is nothing we can do to bring him to account?"

"Nothing," said Holmes shortly.

I made my way downstairs, accompanied by the talkative Boots.

"And Mrs. H has said as how I can help her when she takes things over to Hampstead. Can I take the dog, says I, for a run on the heath? Why not! Says she, as cheerful as may be. Such a turnabout Doctor. You've been a tonic and no mistake. A tonic."

I winced painfully at his choice of words and made my farewell. As I passed through the street door, of a sudden the whole house shook with the reverberations of an almighty crack. Holmes, exuberant with his whip!

No emotions indeed, I thought wryly to myself.

# A Final Tale

## A Final Tale

**Wednesday**

Holmes had a bad night again last night. I took what rest I could in his dressing room, wrapped in a blanket and sitting in an armchair, restlessly listening to his mutterings and cries.

Sometimes he calls for me by name; sometimes his cries are indecipherable. It is impossible for me to know whether he is beset by nightmares or if indeed he is awake and haunted by the confusion which is increasingly frequent.

Once when I was more asleep than awake, I thought I heard him call for Mycroft, dead these many years. Sometimes he has cried out for Mrs. Hudson, also dead this long time. And me, he calls for me.

**Thursday**

He cried out again last night. I heard him call me by name: "Watson? Watson, are you there?"

I went in to him. "Holmes, old man," I said. "I am here, old chap. What can I do for you?"

He said "Tell Lestrade that he is mistaken. There is no accomplice. The young man – oh, but where am I? What is this? Watson, Watson, help me get out of this! Curse this darkness!" He strove against me, and I held him as still as I could, murmuring soothingly to him, hoping his animal distress would calm. There was a time when I would never have held my own in a physical struggle with Holmes, but now he is as weak as a kitten. His wasted frame ceased struggling and he relaxed against my chest. After a few moments he looked up at me and I saw that he was experiencing one of his rare moments of lucidity, for his eyes cleared and looked directly and penetratingly into mine.

"Watson," he said with some urgency, "I beg of you, release me from this horror. My mind is slipping fast. I know what is happening. I can scarcely hold it even now." He reached up and grasped my collar. "You have been my companion these many long years – you know that without my mind I am nothing, nothing! You know that I don't hope for anything beyond. Watson, please help me!"

Then his eyes began to glaze again, and he fixed me with a puzzled, frightened look. "Mycroft? No, you're not Mycroft. Get away, whoever you are, you frighten me."

**Friday**

I dreamt of Mary again last night, as I do most nights, but last night she was accompanied by our daughter. Not as she had been in her short infant life here on earth, but as the young woman she would have been had she lived. I am an old man, and have survived those more worthy than I. I perceive no pattern here, no purpose. When I came back to live with Holmes a twelvemonth ago, I was resigned to we two being old men together, irascible, irritable, perhaps reminiscing about the thrills and the triumphs we have shared – for there have been many – perhaps only arguing about the toast, but I little thought we would descend so quickly into illness and confusion. I find that in all conscience I cannot witness another moment of Holmes begging me for release. It is terrible for me to see in my old friend, once so brilliant, once carrying all before him. Tonight, I take my old bag in with me.

**Saturday**

It is over. I told the doctor who has just left me now that when Holmes woke in the night his anguish was so great that I had no choice but to provide him with a sedative. I said that perhaps in his wasted condition he was materially weakened, and that perhaps the dose of laudanum I gave him was greater than his frame could withstand. I said if that were by any chance the case, I was profoundly sorry.

The doctor – when did the young become wise? – looked me gently in the eye, and putting his hand kindly on my arm, said, "I believe you have been a good friend tonight, Dr. Watson."

Have I been a good friend? I hope I have. Goodbye, old chap.

Also from Orange Pip Books

It is well documented that Sherlock Holmes is the most depicted literary character on screen; he even has an entry in the Guinness Book of Records to prove it. This reference guide covers depictions of the world's most famous detective, and his faithful companion, from the first silent film Sherlock Holmes is Baffled (1900) to the Will Ferrell, John C. Reilly comedy Holmes and Watson (2018). As well as cinema and television portrayals, this book by Nicko Vaughan (Author of The Wordy Companion: An A-Z Guide to Sherlockian Phraseology) also covers documentaries, animations and web series adaptations alongside début feature artwork by graphic artist Georgia Grace Weston.

Combining encyclopaedia, biography and reference structure, this book comprehensively explores the many celluloid faces, cathode-ray shapes and digital sizes of Sherlock Holmes and Doctor John Watson, so far.

Also from Orange Pip Books

Violet Holmes is not an ordinary teenager because, well, nothing is ordinary when you're the adopted daughter of the great Sherlock Holmes. Having been home schooled for her entire life she has decided to take the plunge, at 14, and attend Bardle Secondary School to study for her exams. But after a week, she notices that the school hides a deep secret, and she's determined to crack it wide open. Are the current spate of school thefts the work of criminal masterminds? Is there really a secret society behind closed doors? Can a girl like Violet make friends and fit in?

Also from Orange Pip Books

*Just the place for a Nark!" the Detective cried,*
*As he eagerly surveyed the scene;*
*With the stout-hearted Doctor alert at his side,*
*And the Dog standing guard in between.*

Imagine a world where the logic of Sherlock Holmes meets the nonsense of Wonderland! *The Hunting of the Nark* combines the best of Lewis Carroll and Arthur Conan Doyle's adventures into a madcap collection of verse, including the novella-length case, *The Adventure of the Twinkling Hat*. Holmes and Watson will discover that anything can happen at 221B when you're the White Knight...

Dr. John H. Watson is a man of medical science, a man of action and a man of letters. His life has been one of adventure and romance. In 1894 he finds himself alone following the death of his great friend Sherlock Holmes three years earlier and now the passing of his beloved wife, Mary. His loneliness is all encompassing and only a true friend can help him to see there is still reason to continue living. But when that friend, Inspector G. Lestrade of Scotland Yard suddenly and mysteriously disappears, Dr. Watson takes it upon himself to discover the reason for the abduction.

Also from Orange Pip Books

It wasn't that John couldn't tell the story. It wasn't that we didn't know the truth. It was that nobody would believe us. But we cannot keep Sherlock alive with silence. The reader smiles when Moriarty appears on the page. So does Moriarty. And Sherlock Holmes follows him. We smile because we recognise them. Scarlett Vendalle is recognised by nobody, except for John Watson. With no recollection of her own identity and a suspected criminal past, Scarlett is the perfect case for Sherlock. As they follow her tracks, red threads appear in their lives that make it more than clear - Scarlett meeting John and Sherlock was no coincidence. Someone has drawn her shadow on the wall before she appeared. Was it Anne Boleyn who haunts Scarlett with visions of her past? Was it Moriarty who attracts Sherlock like a magnet? Or was it another shadow from the past? With Moriarty's men on the one hand and the secret service on the other, the stage is set for a game with deadly rules, as Sherlock, John and Scarlett slowly become aware that something larger is guiding their steps...

Is there another story being written?

www.ingramcontent.com/pod-product-compliance
Lightning Source LLC
Chambersburg PA
CBHW070614310726
48982CB00001B/75

*9781804242865*